GW01043919

I was given a copy of BLOODLINE, the first book in their SPELLBOUND CHRONICLES trilogy, by my friends Eve and Suzanne. I began reading it with interest and curiosity which soon turned to an overwhelming desire to find out what happens next. This is an extremely well-written story with a great deal of mystery and suspense, lots of exciting action and a setting that is totally believable despite being a fantasy adventure novel.

The story concerns two teenagers, Larna and Aron Gorry, who visit their grandmother in Sherwood Forest. Almost immediately, they are drawn into an epic struggle between the forces of good and evil taking place in another time-zone. Making friends with a wizard called Balgaire and his family, they battle against the destructive forces of the warlock Mordrog and his sly assistant Edsel. Larna and Aron find themselves in a series of terrifying predicaments that tax their bravery and endurance to the limit.

I found the good characters warm and sympathetic and the bad ones genuinely scary. The story has great pace and there are no slow sections or long passages of description. The action is gripping and has a number of clever twists and genuine surprises along the way. Eve and Suzanne are talented authors and I look forward to reading the other two books in the series when they are written.

I would recommend BLOODLINE to anyone who likes inventive fantasy adventure stories or is just looking for a really good read.

Henry Kingston

SPELLBOUND CHRONICLES

Bloodline

Suzanne and Eve Maguire

Copyright © 2014 Suzanne Maguire and Eve Maguire

The moral right of the author has been asserted.

Apart from any fair dealing for the purposes of research or private study,
or criticism or review, as permitted under the Copyright, Designs and Patents
Act 1988, this publication may only be reproduced, stored or transmitted, in
any form or by any means, with the prior permission in writing of the
publishers, or in the case of reprographic reproduction in accordance with
the terms of licences issued by the Copyright Licensing Agency. Enquiries
concerning reproduction outside those terms should be sent to the publishers.

Matador
9 Priory Business Park
Kibworth Beauchamp
Leicestershire LE8 0RX, UK
Tel: (+44) 116 279 2299
Fax: (+44) 116 279 2277
Email: books@troubador.co.uk
Web: www.troubador.co.uk/matador

ISBN 978 1783064 694

British Library Cataloguing in Publication Data.
A catalogue record for this book is available from the British Library.

Typeset by Troubador Publishing Ltd

Matador is an imprint of Troubador Publishing Ltd

To ALL OUR READERS
Friends and family

And many others for not yawning through the umpteenth re-writes – you know who you are.

Paul Horsman and team at Doncaster Waterstones. Thanks for your endless patience.

Not forgetting Gordon Volke for his invaluable help and encouragement. We certainly needed you.

To Professor Dame Pamela Shaw and team at SITran: for working tirelessly to find a cure for MND/ALS

And finally, our thanks to Amy, Rosie and Jeremy at Troubador.

To Larna and Aron,

Time is running out for us and we desperately need your help.
You are our link against the forces of evil, and our only hope.
Trust Clement for guidance.
We wait in time to meet you.

CHAPTER ONE

Larna Gorry had her recurring dream the night before her mum took her and her younger brother Aron to stay with their grandmother in her cottage deep in Sherwood Forest. She'd had these dreams since her last birthday in March. At first they were okay but a bit confusing. Then, last night, her dream had become more sinister.

It always began with a boy of about her own age, 14, with piercing green eyes and blonde hair scraped back in a ponytail. There was something odd about him that meant he was not entirely human. Larna never felt threatened when the boy beckoned her into his world because she was always able to resist. Except this time. This time it was different. The urgency of the summons seemed desperate and Larna's natural curiosity got the better of her. As she took a step towards him, the relief that registered on the boy's face suddenly changed to fear directed at something over Larna's shoulder. She snapped round to see a dense black shadow rushing towards her. She froze instantly. As she was about to be enveloped by the 'thing', she felt the same fear she saw reflected in the boy's face.

With a jolt, Larna woke up, choking. She began to shake. It was pitch black and deadly quiet, the middle of the night. Sitting bolt upright, she hugged her knees and began to rock. She knew she'd been dreaming, but it had felt so real, leaving her with a nasty feeling of dread. She reached for her half-read book on the bedside cabinet and settled back on the pillows in the hope that a good read would calm her down. She must have fallen asleep because it only seemed a few minutes before she heard her mother, Elizabeth, calling, "Larna! Aron! Time to get out of your pits. You don't want to be late on the last day of term."

Half asleep, she realised it was morning. The light was still on and her book had fallen onto the floor. Kicking away the duvet, she crawled out of bed and made her way to the bathroom before her brother had a chance to hog it. After a quick shower, she knocked on twelve-year-old Aron's door. The only response was a grunt. Par for the course.

Back in her bedroom, Larna was starting to get dressed when she experienced a sudden flashback to last night's nightmare. It sent shivers down her spine. Then, from the bottom of the stairs, her mum broke her dark train of thought and raised her spirits by saying breakfast was ready. Afterwards, once they'd eaten, she took the stairs two at a time, racing Aron back to the bathroom. She spat out the toothpaste and rinsed, then raised her head to inspect her face, making sure she hadn't left any white residue around her mouth. The mirror had steamed up so she used the heel of her right hand to circle a clear patch.

"What the... " she gasped and sprang backwards, hitting the wall. Her heart rate beat at double time as she held onto the towel rail for support. The face in the mirror wasn't hers! She had expected to see her green eyes, straight nose and mousy-brown shoulder-length hair tucked behind her ears. Instead she saw the boy in her nightmare extending his arm to make contact.

"Larna, wake up! Breakfast's ready." Aron was shaking her shoulder. "This is your final call." Larna's eyes sprang open and she was thankful to see her brother instead of the strange boy gazing at her. Relief flooded her mind as she realized it had still been a nightmare all along.

* * *

Back in her room she double-checked the contents of her backpack to make sure she hadn't forgotten anything. "One torch, one notepad, one set of clues, dad's GPS... I'm all set!"

On their last holiday with their father he had introduced them to geocaching, an Americanised treasure hunting game. They'd used a GPS to locate the area where the cache box, full of goodies, lay hidden, but clues were essential to finding its exact position.

If someone decided to remove an item from the container, it was common courtesy to replace it with something else. Larna always carried a school key ring, just in case. She and Aron were looking forward to playing this game again in Sherwood Forest during the holidays.

A car backfiring reminded her that mum was waiting to drive them to school. Grabbing Aron's sleeve she pulled him through the hall and out of the house, banging the door shut behind them. From the outside, Hayfield School was small and compact, but it was deceptive, much like the Tardis in *Dr Who*, Larna had always thought, because on the inside it was astoundingly large. Two floors of corridors led off in all directions to classrooms, study rooms, the library and the dining hall. Even now she still occasionally lost her bearings in the maze.

The morning dragged until the lunch bell echoed through the building. With twenty minutes to kill before her sitting, Mr Waight, her chemistry teacher, suggested Larna should make good use of her time in the library revising part of the lesson she'd had difficulty with. Entering the large, oblong room, Larna realised she was alone. The only movements were particles of dust floating upwards in a shaft of sunlight and the big hand on the clock, as it ticked the seconds away. Locating the reference book, she grabbed it from the shelf and sat down at the nearest table.

Totally immersed in the pages her eyes began to droop. She didn't notice the sudden drop in temperature until an almighty shiver ran through her body and she caught sight of her breath on the cold air. The sun had vanished, plunging the room into semi-darkness which cast eerie shadows all around. Reaching across the table, she switched on the lamp and was immediately confronted by a dense black mass. Fear temporarily rooted her to the chair as she thought she recognised the spectre from her nightmare attempting to envelop her again. In a frantic scramble to escape, the chair flipped backwards taking Larna with it. Her head hit the floor with a terrific bang and she lost consciousness.

She came round to someone, or something, tapping her face in none too gentle a fashion. Confused and disorientated, she opened her eyes and recognised Mr Waight.

"Lie perfectly still, Larna, until I've checked you out. Whatever happened? You had me worried for a while." Not waiting for a reply, he held up four fingers and asked Larna to count them. Then the school nurse arrived and took over. Within a few minutes she had her patient sitting up.

"There doesn't seem to be much wrong with you, but from the noise your stomach is making, I guess you missed your lunch."

Larna nodded dumbly.

"That could be why you fainted." She felt the back of Larna's head and drew in a quick breath. "You'll have a big lump there tomorrow, young lady. Go to the kitchen and have something to eat while I write a note for you to give to your mother."

Larna didn't want to openly disagree with the woman's diagnosis. She'd already concluded that she'd fallen asleep and plunged right back into her nightmare. Mr Waight helped her to her feet and escorted her to the canteen, sitting opposite while she ate, watching every move just to make sure she wasn't suffering from concussion. Eating in silence and still feeling woozy, Larna wondered if her strange dreams were supposed to mean anything.

During the final study period, the nurse gave her a letter for her mum, sealed, so she couldn't read it. Instead of shoving it into her pocket she screwed it up into a tight ball and unobtrusively dropped it into the waste bin. There was no way she was going to worry her mother, or even tell Aron, as they'd only want all the details. For the rest of the afternoon Larna kept checking the classroom clock, desperately willing the hands to get a move on and the final bell to ring. When it did, she shot up, said a quick goodbye to her best friend Jonty and rushed for the door.

"Don't run!" yelled Mr Robertson, her English teacher.

Larna took no notice. Backpack over her shoulder, she was out of the classroom like a bullet, heading for the car park and the great escape.

Aron obviously had the same idea because they bumped into each other on the way out and raced up the path to the gates. Their mum's car was rocking with her loud music blasting out. Much to Larna's relief she turned the volume right down as soon as they slung their bags into the boot. They strapped themselves in whilst their mum neatly manoeuvred the car through the school traffic and they were on their way.

Although there were hold-ups due to road works, they made good time and soon they were turning off the A1 onto Blyth Road, through the gates of Clumber Park and onto an avenue of massive lime trees. Their mum always found her way through this maze of trees and avenues into Sherwood Forest with ease. But this time they hadn't travelled very far into the forest when they found their route blocked. The car skidded to a halt, narrowly missing a huge trunk. Everything that wasn't wedged in or anchored down went flying. Their seat belts saved them from the same fate. Unbuckling, they all got out of the car and looked around. Debris lay in their path.

"What the...?" their mum said. "The weather forecast never mentioned this."

"What are we going to do if we can't get through?"

"I'll have to find another way, Aron. But... "

At that precise moment the three of them were startled by the sudden appearance of an elderly man with an unruly shock of red hair. Elizabeth gave a little squeal. Aron and Larna also jumped.

"Whoa! Where did you come from?" Larna asked.

The man pointed into the woods. "There's my hut so, I expect that's where I came from." He took off his funny flat cap and held it humbly with both hands. Then he turned to their mum. "I'm sorry if I frightened you, Mrs."

"No harm done, Mr... ?"

"Clem. Short for Clement – unlike the weather we've had of late, don't ya know." He smiled, showing two huge fangs which sent a shot of anxiety through Larna and Aron.

"If you are going to Miss Neve's, will you tell her... " he turned his back on the youngsters before finishing.

Half covering her mouth Larna whispered, "How does he know where we're going?"

Aron shrugged and pulled a face. "I don't know."

While the grown-ups chatted, the two youngsters studied him. "Clem? That's a peculiar name," Aron commented, looking to his sister for confirmation of his observation.

"Ssshh, he'll hear."

Aron kicked the debris at his feet. "I've never seen hair that red before. Look how it sticks up."

"I've never seen a woodsman wearing green tights either," Larna whispered back. "Do you think he realises we can see them under his long black mac?"

"Don't know. He's a strange old bod. He reminds me of a sort of medieval vampire. He'd be right at home in one of those old movies."

Aron was right. He was ancient and slightly bent, as though not used to standing straight anymore. He was a funny-looking old man who appeared scary at first but who was obviously just trying to help. Elizabeth nodded to her children to get back into the car. She shook Clem's hand, got in herself and buckled up, instructing them to do the same. Winding down the window she said, "Thank you, Clement, you've been most helpful. I promise I will pass your message on to my mother." He gave an exaggerated salute with his right hand as he clutched his cap in his left. "You're very kind don't ya know, Mrs." He looked directly at Larna and Aron in the back and acknowledged them with a salute too. As their mum reversed the car, manoeuvring it onto another path, Larna turned and looked out of the window. Clem was still in the same spot, watching.

"In all these years I didn't know this path existed. You live and learn," said their mum. Glancing through the rear window again a blink later, Larna found Clem and his hut had vanished. All that was left was a large black crow staring back at her.

* * *

Following the old man's instructions to the letter, it didn't take long to re-join their usual route into Sherwood. They'd only lost about twenty minutes by going round the fallen trees.

"I can't understand it," said mum.

"Me neither. It's weird." agreed Larna

"What is?" Aron asked.

"It looked as if that one spot has been hit by a tornado.

Nowhere else. Very strange. Still, no harm done. We're on the right road now." She drove in silence after that.

Relaxing into the corner of the car, Larna shut her eyes and let her thoughts drift. She realised this would be their first geocache without dad organising it. She hoped they wouldn't make a mess of it. Glancing sideways at Aron, it struck her how much he looked like their father with his dark blonde curly hair and button nose, even though he possessed their mum's sky-blue eyes. Aron's cheeky grin though was all his own, and it had often got him into – and out of – trouble.

Ten minutes later they turned right onto familiar territory and into their comfort zone. The sight of their grandmother's quirky white cottage always perked Larna up and today was no exception. There was something mystical about the old building. Larna always felt like it was trapped in a time warp and she loved it. The drive was lined with ancient oaks, like sentries forming a guard of honour, with a sea of bluebells between each one.

Without warning, a strong wind blew, coming at them from both left and right, rocking the car from side to side. Then, just as suddenly, it changed tack as if it couldn't make up its mind. As Larna strained to see the sky from the safety of her seat, she noticed that the bluebells were bowed towards her, all in the one direction, and yet the wind was still swirling erratically through everything else around. This was also weird, but she quickly forgot about it. They had arrived at their grandmother's. Larna hadn't realised just how much she'd missed the old place. Nothing had changed since their last visit and she felt a little splurge of excitement, but at the same time had a strange feeling that something was different – slightly off-kilter.

Their grandmother – known in the family as Yaya – must have heard the tyres on the gravel as they approached. She came rushing out waving frantically, clearly as excited as they were. The car hadn't even fully stopped when Aron and Larna jumped out in their enthusiasm to be the first to receive one of her massive hugs. They weren't disappointed. Apart from her long blonde hair and blue eyes like her daughter, Neve was a bit of a mystery. To friends and family she was loving, kind, protective and full of fun.

She encouraged her grandchildren's adventurous spirit (as she always called it). But to others, she appeared a bit standoffish and reclusive. Even 'regal' had been whispered once or twice by those who were totally in awe of her.

Yaya Neve drew Larna and Aron either side of her and gave them another quick squeeze whilst winking at their mum. "Missed both of you. Far too quiet when you're not here to run me ragged."

Aron squirmed when she mussed his hair. She gave her grandson a playful push and said, "Aha! Too old for that now, I expect. Go on then, get your things out of the car. I presume you're staying."

The two of them were chuffed to be back, even though Aron tried not to show it. They hoicked their backpacks out of the boot and banged it shut. Aron beat Larna to Neve this time and, with an arm round both of them, she led them into the cottage. Ten minutes later, Elizabeth was pouring tea into two white china mugs and handing one to her mother. "It's good of you to have these two, I really appreciate it. They've promised to behave like mature adults and get on together."

"Is that so?" Neve chuckled.

Aron gave her one of his looks, "Aw, now you've taken all the fun out of it."

While they were drinking and chatting, Larna noticed how similar the two women's mannerisms were. They were obviously very close, especially since Pompa Douglas (grandpa) died just before Aron was born. A feeling of sadness swept over her as she realised Yaya Neve had been alone all those years, although she was certain she'd heard her grandmother talking to him from time to time. Worryingly she'd also thought she'd heard him reply. Larna pulled out of her daydream in time to hear her mum finish the story of their detour in the woods.

"I've never experienced anything like it. It was just in that area as if somebody was deliberately putting obstacles in our way. If it weren't for Clem... oh, he gave me a message for you." She paused, wrinkling her brow. "He said it was very urgent and to be sure I repeat it verbatim – when you're on your own." She gave Larna and Aron a meaningful look.

After a significant pause, without taking her eyes off her daughter, Neve said, "Take your things upstairs, you two, and settle in. You'll soon find your rooms."

As Larna bent to pick up her backpack from where she'd dropped it in the hall, she noticed something strange through the open door. An unusually large black crow stood on the front step studying her. But once eye contact had been made, it upped and flew to the rear of the cottage where the garden met the woods. With nobody else around to notice, her thoughts returned to her grandmother and the message her mum had for her. Aron had already gone upstairs, so Larna tiptoed past the kitchen door, trying not to disturb the grown-ups, but she overheard her mum say, "... that's exactly what he said, word for word – that it can't wait any longer. What did he mean?"

"Nothing! Just the ramblings of an old man, dear. I expect he'll have forgotten it by tomorrow."

"But he was so worried." She gave a little laugh. "A bit melodramatic mind you – shades of *Up Pompeii* and 'Beware the Ides of March.' " She made a slight noise. "I shouldn't laugh. He sounded so sincere."

"No, dear, we shouldn't laugh, he... "

Larna crept up the stairs, keeping to one side in case they creaked. They'd been designated two smaller bedrooms in a part of the cottage she didn't even know existed. Each had the appropriate name on the door. Larna was relieved. At long last she had a room of her own to crash out in. Throwing the heavy backpack onto the bed, she stood and had a quick look round. It was a light and airy room with things painted on the walls, and a great view of the forest from her window. In fact all the rooms had awesome views. She crossed the landing to Aron's room. The walls here were painted from floor to ceiling with murals of Sherwood – a cross between medieval and futuristic themes. The window wall boasted an eye-catchingly realistic scene depicting people huddled round a roaring campfire trying to keep warm on a cold night. Everyone seated was wrapped in what looked like old blankets, while those moving towards the fire had their outer clothes pulled tightly round their bodies.

Flinging herself onto Aron's bed, Larna put her hands behind her head and looked up at the ceiling, "Wow!" she exclaimed. It was painted as a night sky, full of brightly shining stars. She darted to the window and shut the curtains before lying back on the bed to lose herself in the awesome indoor sky. With the curtains pulled together, the huge bonfire scene was complete. Draught from the old window frame moved the curtains, making the flames look so realistic, Larna truly believed she could feel the heat radiating from them. Without thinking she held out her hands to the fire for warmth, then remonstrated with herself. "Don't be stupid, that's impossible!" she chuckled under her breath.

After putting his few clothes away, Aron decided to join his sister on the bed, top-and-tail fashion.

"What's your room like?"

"A bit like this, only I don't think it has as many fancy paintings as yours. I'm going to have another look and unpack. Coming?" Larna swung her legs over the side of the bed.

"No, I think I'll lie here for a bit." He gave Larna a little push with his feet.

Re-crossing the landing, Larna stopped and listened. Her mum and grandmother were still talking, but not loud enough for her to hear what they were saying. Continuing on into her room, she quietly shut the door. Looking again, she saw her wall paintings were actually totally different from her brother's. She inspected them closer and concluded that they looked like creations from another world. Animals, but with a human presence. What a fantastic imagination the artist must have had to paint a scene like this, she thought. There were trees, but none resembling those on Aron's walls. In fact, on reflection, Larna thought her brother's bedroom had a much darker theme than hers.

Examining the room further, her gaze was drawn to the right hand wall and to a quaint old cottage with blue-grey smoke curling from an unusual spiral chimney. In front of it, and what grabbed her attention, was a larger-than-life wizard, complete with long robe and a tall hat, but with no magic wand in his hand.

Moving away to inspect the other two walls, she felt a slight tug and a feather-light tap on her back which made her jump and turn round. Nobody else was in the room. Fixing her gaze on the wizard eyeball-to-eyeball, she found herself asking if he could've just touched her. Then she sat down on the bed and said out loud, "What am I doing? I'm talking to a brick wall!"

There were no paintings on the wall at the foot of the bed. Instead, it had a wash of calming green, as if the artist had run out of ideas and put down his brushes, never to return. Putting her clothes away, Larna couldn't shake off the feeling she wasn't alone; she was sure she could feel the wizard's eyes trailing her every move. She put it down to a trick of the light. There's always a straight answer to everything, she told herself, although she wasn't entirely convinced. The spell was immediately broken when their grandmother called upstairs that their mum was ready to leave and they'd better make haste if they wanted to say goodbye.

Elizabeth and Yaya were in the garden finishing their tea. It wasn't a particularly large garden, but it was Neves pride and joy. She'd often said that the perfume from her early border roses filled the air and just a few deep breaths made her want to slow down and enjoy her surroundings. At the bottom of the garden a rickety old gate painted glossy green marked the boundary. Their grandmother had told them that in the dead of night, when the moon was full, the gate would glow and act as a beacon showing Yaya the way home. What a load of rubbish, Larna thought. It had never occurred to her to ask what their grandmother was doing in the woods at midnight... alone.

CHAPTER TWO

The woods had always had an eerie fascination for Larna and her brother. Some of the trees were so old she often amused herself with thoughts of the stories and dark tales they could tell if they could talk. And paths leading to places who knows where. Being strictly forbidden, these were an almost irresistible temptation.

As the children were growing up, a strict embargo was put on going through the gate. No amount of pleading would change their grandmother's mind, even when they promised on their pet hamster Snowy's life not to go very far. They never found out why. And they didn't disobey. Years ago Larna had frightened the life out of Aron with horror stories about what would happen if they didn't do as they were told and somehow she'd begun to believe them herself.

Taking a final sip of tea, their mum looked up and, in her serious voice that she saved for important family announcements, said, "I know your father feels you are more responsible now and has lent you his GPS. So I've decided I'm going to give my permission for you to explore the woods surrounding the cottage. With one proviso – on *no* account must you separate or lose sight of one another. Okay? But Yaya has the final say."

Larna and Aron turned to Neve with bated breath. Biting her bottom lip, she looked worried about something, hesitating before replying in their favour. They nearly dropped from shock. Finding their voices, they couldn't thank either of them enough, repeating themselves so many times that their mum reached up and put her hands over their mouths to shut them up. Then she looked at her watch and gasped.

"Time always seems to fly when I'm here." She stood up and

smoothed her dress, then opened her arms for a final hug. Larna gave her a squeeze and stepped sideways to give Aron a turn. Aron hung back as usual. In the end he mumbled something about missing her.

"Love you," Larna said.

"Ditto," replied Mum.

And from Aron, a simple, "Me too!"

She picked up her keys and they followed her to the car. "Remember your promise, Aron, not to annoy your sister."

"So long as she doesn't annoy me!"

"As if I would! I'm the grown-up one, remember?"

"Yeah, right. With a teddy bear on your bed at home... "

"That's enough!" scolded Mum She turned to Aron. "No trouble, okay?"

"Okay?"

"Sorry, I didn't hear that."

"I promise!" he said, looking her straight in the eye.

After giving Neve a final hug their mum got into the car, lowered the window and gave Larna a knowing wink. She nodded. Their secret code for "look after your brother." As she pulled away, she stuck her arm out of the car and waved all the way down the tree lined drive. They all watched until she turned right and vanished from sight.

* * *

Neve and Aron took the path round the cottage to the back door. Larna watched them go, listening to her brother grumbling about his empty stomach. "I'm starving. What've you got, Yaya?"

"Didn't take long for you to start thinking about food," came the faint reply.

Larna went in the front door. Pausing on the step for a few minutes in the gathering gloom, she wondered how far they'd be allowed to explore in the morning. Her brain began to work overtime and a tingle of excitement took hold, as she planned the cache hunt. Suddenly she was distracted by a peculiar whooshing sound. She looked up too quickly and her head began to swim.

Coming straight towards her was that same black menacing 'thing' from her nightmares. She dropped to the floor in a half-curl, covered her head with her arms, held her breath and waited. Whatever it was had found her again. This time, though, she wasn't dreaming. What on earth was happening here?

Silence. Cautiously she raised her head. The shape was nowhere to be seen and, although shaken, to her amazement she was totally unharmed. She breathed a huge sigh of relief. But what to do next? Should she tell Yaya? Would she even believe her? Mum would only think she was making it up to scare Aron. The thoughts raced through Larna's head. She decided just to keep it to herself for now.

On shaky legs and not wishing to be alone any longer, she hurried to find the others. Her stomach growled loudly and she didn't need a list of clues to follow the savoury smells through the front hall and on into the kitchen. When her plate was placed in front of her, she discovered that her appetite had vanished. Along with the spectre.

Time seemed to fly after dinner. Banished to the sitting room, Larna and Aron watched television until boredom set in, then flipped through a couple of books Neve had left out. The earthy smell from the fire in the ingle-nook made them drowsy and before they knew it, their eyes became heavy and they dozed. Then the old grandfather clock boomed ten, shattering the silence and waking them up. After the day she'd had Larna couldn't believe she'd managed to even grab a light doze.

Neve was sitting in her chair gazing out of the window, her brow furrowed, deep in thought. "You two have missed a glorious sunset. I hope it bodes well for tomorrow." She turned and gave them a worried smile. "I have a funny feeling about this particular holiday." Raising her face, she sniffed. "There's something different in the air tonight." Then she shook her head. "Enough of my meandering. Time for bed. Lights out in fifteen and *no* talking. My bedroom is close and I have big ears."

The young guests headed upstairs and separated on the landing, too tired to say anything but, "Night." As usual Aron grunted and closed his bedroom door. He never needed rocking and would no doubt be asleep before his head hit the pillow. Normally Larna was not far behind him, but tonight was different, no doubt because of her earlier encounter. She still couldn't get her head round it. There must be a logical explanation.

For her own sanity she decided to push it out of her mind, well at least as far to the back as it would go, and then she focussed her thoughts on what they would find beyond the gate. She snuggled further down the welcoming bed. The book she had brought still lay unopened on the bedside cabinet. Turning off the lamp, she pulled the old fashioned quilt up and nestled it under her chin. She lay looking up at the ceiling. The blue sky and puffy clouds that had adorned her ceiling in the daylight had been replaced with shimmering stars like Aron's. They were mesmerising, and as she gazed she could feel herself being slowly drawn into a much-needed slumber. The room began to fade as she felt herself drifting... drifting...

Her dreams made no sense at first, flitting erratically from one scene to another, but eventually her mind cleared and out of the fog came a new vision. A different time. She wasn't sure how she got there. She vaguely remembered searching for the cache with her dad's clues. She began to explore. The trees around her seemed familiar. She paused. Stood very still and looked around. Then it hit her. These trees were identical to the ones painted on her bedroom walls. But where was she? The ground was covered with fallen leaves. She picked one up. It was a bizarre shade of purple with a sweet smell that reminded her of watermelons. Letting the leaf drift back to the ground, she continued her journey.

Lost in thought and wonder, she felt a gentle tap on her shoulder. Without thinking, she brushed it off. A much harder tap took her by surprise and she jumped round. She found herself face-to-face with the boy from her dreams. He stood motionless in front of her and Larna studied him. He was unlike anyone she'd ever seen before. His nose was black and shiny and, poking through his long hair, were what appeared to be the tips of partly formed dog's ears. They stared at each other for a few seconds, then Larna put out a hand to touch him, to prove he wasn't a figment of her imagination. The boy had the same idea. As they simultaneously stretched out their fingers, Larna held her breath and waited for their fingertips to meet. The two hands passed over each other, but Larna felt nothing. She tried again, shaking but determined. Still no contact. It must be a ghost. It was the only possible conclusion.

"You are Larna?"

* * *

There was an irritating buzz in Larna's ear. Her watch. Its alarm was making a racket fit to wake the rest of the house. She pushed it under the pillow until it stopped. Rubbing her eyes with the heels of her hands, she breathed a sigh of relief, realising that the trees and the canine boy had all been a powerful dream.

Throwing off the covers, she jumped out of bed and partially opened the curtains. She was greeted by a glorious day. The first of their few days holiday, and freedom. She pulled her watch from under the pillow; nine o'clock She shook her head, certain she'd set the alarm for eight. Oh well, the extra hour will have done me good, she concluded. There wasn't a sound from Aron's room. Nothing unusual in that, though.

Neve was already at the kitchen table engrossed in a newspaper with a cup of tea to her lips. Larna's favourite cereal, a bowl, a jug of milk and a glass of freshly squeezed orange juice (without the bits) indicated her place. A similar arrangement of Aron's favourites was across from hers. Larna took a huge helping, drank the juice and wiped her mouth on a piece of kitchen roll. In record time she had thanked her grandmother and made her escape upstairs to see if Aron had surfaced. Up, washed and already dressed, Aron ran past Larna heading for the stairs. Larna turned and was close on his heels. Neve had taken her second cup of tea into the garden to inspect the roses. Larna watched as she appeared to be talking to herself and nodding at the replies. As she wandered further down the garden, Larna shared her crazy dream with Aron.

Her brother ignored her and continued stuffing his face with chocolate cereal. Larna hated it when he did that. Eventually he put down his spoon, finished his apple juice, wiped his mouth on the back of his hand, leaned over the table and looked Larna dead in the eye.

"What are you going on about now, sis?"

"Haven't you heard a word... too busy scoffing... I said... "

"I *heard* what you said. Some nonsense about weird trees and a boy who looks like a dog. I've heard it before." He pulled a funny face and waggled his fingers in a mock-scary manner. "What're you gonna dream up next, eh?"

Larna was not about to give her brother the satisfaction of knowing he'd succeeded in rattling her cage or goading her into a reply. Then Neve entered the kitchen and Larna just made it to Aron's side in time. He grinned at Larna. "Yaya. Larna says... " Her right hand shot up and clamped his mouth. At the same time, her left hand grabbed the back of Aron's top and dragged him outside.

"Just a bit of fun. Can't you take a joke?"

"Stop it now!" yelled their grandmother. "Remember your promise!" Her voice carried through the cottage like a loudspeaker. I bet mum didn't get away with much when she was growing up, thought Larna. Sometimes she thought Gran had eyes in the back of her head and radar-flapping ears. So the two of them cleared the table, put the dishes in the dishwasher and then raced each other up the stairs, the dream and Aron's taunts forgotten.

* * *

Teeth hastily done, the GPS, clues and key-ring safely hidden in Larna's pockets, she joined her brother in the panelled hall. It always smelled of lavender polish and gleamed from years of TLC. The grandfather clock began to strike ten. Having successfully banished the spectre to the back of her mind, Larna patted her pocket and nodded. Keeping her promise to their mum, she felt a keen responsibility for Aron's safety as well as her own. But what harm could come to them on a bright sunny day if they stuck together?

Neve's empty cup was placed on the table next to her neatly

folded newspaper. The back door being wide open, it didn't need Einstein's brain to work out that she had returned to the garden. They found her feeding the birds and topping up their water bowls and tubes of peanuts and seed. Balanced on the garden gate, Larna noticed another unusually large black crow. Could it be the same one from yesterday? As she watched, it appeared to be staring straight back at her. Full of confidence, not frightened, challenging even.

The staring competition was abruptly halted as Larna was distracted by her Gran putting the spare seed back in the garden shed. She'd been talking to the pair of them for a quite a while, but Larna hadn't heard a word.

"I have to go out for a while, I'm afraid. The pantry and freezer need restocking." She glanced at her watch. "I shouldn't be too long. You'll be fine on your own for a while, won't you?"

Aron and Larna exchanged looks. "We'll find something to do, Yaya, don't you worry." Aron told her. "Take your time, have a cuppa and a cream bun while you're at it."

She smiled. "I'll be home for one o'clock to make lunch. So if you go out, please be back by then."

"Okay," they chorused.

"How far can we go, and can we use the GPS?" Larna asked eagerly.

"I'd prefer that you waited until I return. Just an added precaution, for your safety. After all, you don't understand yet what could be out there."

"How far can we go *without* the GPS, then?" Aron was insistent.

"No further than the big tree," was the very definite response as she pointed into the woods. Aron scrunched his face and said sarcastically, "Which big tree Gran? Can you be more specific, there are so many."

She smiled, "You will recognise it. It's big, it's very old and gnarled. Unlike any other. It has peculiar shaped dark green leaves right at the top. You can't miss it. In fact, if you concentrate very hard on the trunk, it has been known for a person to see a face in the bark staring back."

"Why, though? Why not past that tree?" Aron grumbled.

"Just to be on the safe side. If anything happened to you, I'd never forgive myself. Your mother wouldn't either. And just because... " Disappointment was painted across their young faces, "I'm sorry, I know how frustrated you must feel and you were looking forward to exploring the area. But I have very good reasons why you shouldn't wander so far while I'm out."

Aron pouted. "What possible reason could there be?"

"I'm afraid you'll just have to accept my judgement and ruling on this." She was quite firm this time. They knew to leave it at that.

Neve picked up her bag and car keys from the hall stand and the two of them followed her out to the garage in front of the shed. "If you do go out, make sure the doors are locked." She took the key out of the lock and showed it to them. "Then put the key in the old tin box under the seat in the back porch."

Larna picked it up and rattled it. There were keys inside for many doors. "Don't you ever get confused?"

"No, but unwanted guests do. Trust me."

Completely covered with variegated ivy, the garage was perfectly camouflaged and when she hit a button hidden by the foliage on the wall, the door slid silently up-and-over. Easing herself into a small red open-top MG, she reversed out of the ancient building.

"Remember you two, if you do leave the garden, promise on your honour that you'll stay together. Under *no* circumstances separate." Her voice and eyes warned them she was deadly serious. They agreed without a murmur. With a final nod of approval, she released the hand-brake and as she drove away the garage door quietly returned to its disguise as an overgrown hedge.

Larna and Aron walked round to the front of the cottage and watched the little red sports car until it reached the end of the drive, turned right and disappeared out of sight.

CHAPTER THREE

Silence, except for the birds and rustle of ornamental grass as a slight breeze caught it. Sitting on the bench in the garden contemplating how soon they could use the GPS, Aron turned his head and looked at his sister. A smile tipped the corner of his lips, slowly pulling them into a wide grin. They stared at each other for a few seconds, then simultaneously scrambled up and ran to lock the back door, their grandmother having already done the front. They put the key in the tin box and pulled on jackets that hung in the back porch.

With a "Let's go!" from Aron, they made what their mum would call an unseemly dash for the garden gate. In spite of jostling each other, they reached it together and grabbed the top bar. Just as quickly they let go, as if they'd received a mild electric shock. It looked very heavy but in actual fact was as light as a feather. It creaked open in slow motion of its own accord. Larna felt great excitement, but it was tainted with a touch of guilt because this was the very first time they were about to deceive Yaya. She pulled out the GPS and held it up to see which direction they'd have to take. It faced north, the way their grandmother had pointed.

"Will we keep going if the cache is further than the boundary tree, Larna?"

"I'm not sure, what do you think?"

"Can't see any harm if it's not much further." He glanced back. "I mean, Yaya's not here so she won't know, will she?"

"Good point." Larna began to weaken. "You never know. The cache could be on this side of the tree, anyway."

"So there's no reason to stop us finding out then, is there?"

Larna gave in. It hadn't taken much to persuade her.

As they moved through the gate, Larna saw the crow again in the middle of the path, watching. She patted the side of her leg hoping it would come to her, but no. It stood as still as a statue, just a few feet away, and as Larna walked towards it, it took off in the direction they were going. She wished she knew the *real* reason why they weren't supposed to go too far from Yaya's cottage. The restriction had put a slight downer on things, especially given the emptiness she felt at not having their dad there to guide them.

Larna took her father's envelope out of her pocket and opened it. The clues were printed clearly on a single white sheet folded in the middle. Needing two hands to read the note, she asked Aron to look after the GPS for a minute. After a brief read of the clues, she focused on the GPS that Aron was holding out in front of them. Still pointing in the direction of the boundary tree, she had a final battle with her conscience. In the end Larna decided it was all or nothing.

"Okay, come on then!" They took their first steps through the brightly painted gate together and entered the wood, side-by-side like a couple of conspirators. Larna noticed that the ground was trodden down, almost flattened in places. "Doesn't look much like unchartered territory to me," she commented as they proceeded with their mission.

There seemed to be not more than four types of trees and lots of birds flying around, chirruping. Larna smiled. They didn't seem to have a care in the world, though she knew nature could be very harsh to the unwary. Some soared upwards, turned and swooped down almost to the ground. She had no idea what they were called. Then a blackbird landed on the path, right in front of them. Any closer and it would've been crushed underfoot with her next step! They had to stop dead. Larna didn't think it realised they were there at first. After pulling a stubborn worm out of the ground, it flew off with its next meal.

They ploughed through some wild honeysuckle, their mum's favourite flower, its scent filling the air and reminding Larna how much she would be enjoying this. They walked slowly for about two minutes, following the GPS and the clues from the list. But the cache wasn't where they thought it would be. Disappointed they began again, going further into Sherwood. It took them another five minutes' search to find a tree which resembled their grandmother's 'big tree.' They sat down either side of it, studying the patterns in the bark. Yes, yes! Larna thought she could definitely see a face and she tilted her head slightly to the right to confirm it. Aron came and sat on the grass next to her and proceeded to point out a different face he'd spotted when he squinted his left eye a little.

"This has got to be it! Now what?"

"I don't know. Want to go on, or turn back?"

Aron's face dropped at this second suggestion. "Carry on as planned!" he exclaimed. "At least until we reach the place where it's buried." When Larna didn't comment he continued, "Don't forget, we can always change our minds at any time – but *not* right now."

So, throwing caution to the wind, that's what they did. They continued walking for another few minutes until they reached the place where the clues kicked in. Turning, the big tree could still be seen. (Well it would have been if you looked in a straight line and could see through a solid mass of trees, that is.) In any event, they'd gone further than they'd anticipated. Aron glanced at his watch and urged, "Hurry up, it'll soon be time to go back."

Holding up the paper, Larna cleared her throat and read, "Look for a mound of large stones. Ten yards to the right, two tree stumps close together. Then twenty yards north of the tree stumps we will find a circle of trees different from all the others. Once located, we've to stand in the centre and there we will find the cache."

They continued their search. A few minutes later Aron shouted that he'd spotted the mound. To be more precise, it was a heap of rocks about knee-high, carefully stacked stone upon stone. Giving each other a high five, they felt elated and couldn't wait to follow the next clue, all thoughts of their promise to Yaya gone with the wind.

"Okay. Now, ten yards to the left."

"How far is that in metres and centimetres?" Aron asked innocently.

"Three feet in a yard and ten times three is what, Aron? You work it out."

Aron laughed. "Just testing."

They walked on until Larna felt a tingling sensation and knew they were getting close.

"Great. This is easier than I thought." Aron said.

Larna was first to spot the two tree stumps and ran towards them. "Now we're supposed to look for a circle... " she murmured, walking north of the two felled trees and counting her steps. "One. Two. Three. Four... " Soon she reached an area that was different. A clearing surrounded by trees.

"I'm sure this is it." Frowning, it all seemed so familiar. "I don't believe this!" Larna blurted out. "Pinch me, Aron."

"What? Why?"

"Just do it!" Larna thought for a second, "On the other hand, don't. Knowing you, it'll hurt too much and leave a bruise."

"I thought it was supposed to." His grin told his sister he would have enjoyed it. "Don't you start going weird on me again, Larna."

"Remember me telling you about my dream last night?"

"I was busy eating if you remember. Anyway, what about it?"

"All this was in my dream. That's why I asked you to pinch me in case I was still asleep." Unable to keep the astonishment out of her voice, she opened her arms to the trees.

"Don't be stupid, Larna. You must have been here before, with Yaya or Mum."

Aron was seriously beginning to annoy Larna. "I have *not!*" she insisted. Then she looked at the clues again. "This is definitely the right place." Walking to the centre of the clearing, she turned to look at her brother. Little shocks of electricity made the hair on the back of her neck and arms stand on end as she felt a rush of adrenalin. She knew the cache was somewhere in the circle – but where? It hadn't been made easy. The ground was covered with layer upon layer of newly fallen leaves. Odd really, considering it was late spring.

Both of them hunted anywhere they thought a cheap plastic box could be hidden. Only when Aron kicked up a pile of leaves and stubbed his big toe did they find what they were looking for inside a partially buried, hollowed-out log. The corner of a red object stuck out. Larna bent down, swept away the rest of the leaves and pulled out a heavy box with an ornamental lid. Not the usual type, this was a heavy metal one. A streak of golden sunlight shone on it and they gasped as it began to glow a blazing red through the dirt. Aron was so excited his knees buckled, dropping him to the ground next to his sister. After a few seconds staring at it, Larna plucked up courage and slowly lifted the lid.

What a disappointment! There was only a rusty old key and a piece of thick yellowed paper which looked as if it had been ripped from a book. No log-book, items or goodies left by previous hunters. Maybe we're the first, Larna thought, picking up the key and rubbing it down the front of her jacket. Its weight surprised her. On closer inspection it was the same shade of red as the box, and the faster she polished, the more details became visible. As sunlight struck the shaft, she saw that the widest part was encrusted with red gem stones, sending off sparkling rays in all directions.

"Now *that's* impressive". Aron said in awe.

He picked up the note and began to read. Larna guessed something was up because he changed colour and pulled a worried face. Without another word Aron thrust the paper into Larna's hands. As she read it out loud and clear, a spike of fear shot through her chest.

To Larna and Aron,

Time is running out for us and we desperately need your help. You are our link against the forces of evil, and our only hope. Trust Clement for guidance. We wait in time to meet you.

CHAPTER FOUR

O ut of total disbelief, Larna was unable to read any further, but after a few minutes she recovered her composure and tried to reason it out.

"It's probably somebody's idea of a joke," she muttered with a false sense of bravado. "But then nobody knows we're here – only Yaya. And she wouldn't frighten us like this, would she?" (More of a statement than a question.) "I doubt it's Dad's doing. He's the only other one I can think of."

"Let's have some fun and solve the mystery, Larna. Come on, what can possibly happen?" Aron grinned, but sensing his sister's shock he tried a different tack. "Besides, what have we got to lose? We've come this far! Go on, Larna, where's your adventurous spirit?" Larna saw him slyly crossing his fingers behind his back. It ruined the moment.

Seemingly from nowhere, and yet from all around, an irate voice said, "Oh *do* make your mind up, Larna! We haven't got all day. I have to agree with Aron, though I take issue on the fun. This is a very serious matter."

Together they gasped, "Who said that?"

"Look up and to your right, you will see who," came the reply. Looking upwards and shading their eyes with their hands, the two of them strained their necks to see where the voice was coming from.

"All I can see is that dumb black crow again," said Aron, shrugging his shoulders.

"I strongly object! I am neither taciturn, stupid nor uncommunicative! And I am certainly *not* dumb, don't you know." The voice was put out. Annoyed.

They jumped back in shock, their jaws dropping fast as they

suddenly realised it *was* the crow talking. They were in eye-to-eye contact with the creature they'd seen in their grandmother's garden. Dropping the note and key, Larna freaked out, overwhelmed. What was happening to them? Grabbing Aron's elbow, she ran like mad, all the way back to the cottage, too scared to make a sound in case they were being chased by demons. Aron followed, close on her heels. They didn't even stop to shut the gate. Nobody had followed them, not even the crow.

They reached the back door and bent down, hands on their knees, out of breath but safe.

"What just happened, Larna?"

"I'm not sure."

"Crows can't talk. But somebody did." Aron paused. "Or something did."

"Could we have touched something that caused us to hallucinate?"

"It's possible. We picked up those strange leaves just before we heard the voice."

Straightening up and stretching her neck to get rid of the crick, Larna started to feel a bit stupid. "I'm not really sure what we heard now, Aron, but I'll be jiggered if it's going to put me off." After three unexplained occurrences – being attacked in the school library by a dark spectre, the spectre returning on her grandmother's front door step and now confronted by a talking crow – you would have expected Larna to be put off from investigating any further. But her natural curiosity sometimes got the better of her. And for once, her brother agreed with her.

"Me neither," he said.

Aron passed the GPS back to Larna who quickly shoved it in her trouser pocket. Then Aron opened the door, holding it for his sister to walk through. As she passed, Aron gently pushed her into the kitchen and towards the table. Looking round, Larna realised Yaya must have returned early because shopping bags were on the work surfaces. Pulling out two chairs they sat down heavily. Elbows on the polished surface, chins in hands, they were silent for what felt like forever. Soft music playing on the radio soothed them, and they could hear her upstairs, presumably tidying up after them. Their mum was always on their case about leaving things lying around in their bedrooms.

As their grandmother made her way down the stairs, Larna suddenly pushed herself away from the table and whispered in Aron's ear, "Better hide the GPS." Then she tried to look innocent as she dashed past the old lady on the stairs, heading to her room. The bed was already made so she took care not to ruffle the covers as she tucked the GPS under her pillow. Standing in the middle of the room she stared at the three painted walls. One of them seemed slightly different, but for the life of her she couldn't tell which one, or what had altered. A shiver went up her spine. She sat on the edge of the bed and wondered if they should ask her gran the meaning of it all and risk being grounded for the rest of the holiday. Larna didn't know which would be worse, banned from going through the gate or the embarrassment of being laughed at and told they'd imagined everything. Or they'd touched something poisonous and hallucinated. That would lead to some of Neve's nasty-tasting homemade herbal medicine. In the end, discretion won the battle and she decided to keep it a secret. For the moment, anyway.

CHAPTER FIVE

"How did your exploration go this morning?" asked their grandmother as they sat round the table after lunch.

"Fine, thanks," answered Larna, shooting a look at her brother to warn him not to give anything away.

"Did you see the faces in the old tree?"

"We did indeed," said Aron with a rather false chuckle. "We looked hard and both of us saw different faces."

"Tea, Yaya?" asked Larna, getting up and reaching for the kettle.

Neve didn't notice they were changing the subject.

"Mm, that would be very welcome," she said. "No sugar and not much milk, please."

The rest of the day was endless. Larna and Aron were bursting to get back into the forest and find out more about the mysterious goings-on of earlier. But they couldn't get away, not with Yaya there. She might have agreed to another short outing from the cottage, but the time they needed to get back to the stone circle where they'd found the note and talked to the crow was much more than she'd be prepared to give them. So they were stuck. Larna tried to pass the time by reading a book in the garden, but she couldn't concentrate on the words. Her mind kept wandering back to the strange events of the morning, question after question turning over in her mind like washing in a tumble-dryer. So she just sat and watched Neve pottering around in the flowerbeds. The old lady seemed not to notice the dark clouds that had gathered in the sky, blotting out the sun and creating a strange eerie light that gave Larna a sense of foreboding, as if something evil was about to happen. Maybe the weather was often like this in Sherwood. Aron didn't notice it, either. He'd made himself comfortable in the kitchen with his MP3 plugged into his ears and an episode of *The Simpsons* on Neve's old-fashioned portable television. Multi-tasking, he called it. Being a moron was what Larna called it.

At last it was time for dinner. Larna didn't feel very hungry. Her guilty conscience about keeping Yaya in the dark and her frustration at not being able to find out anything more took away her appetite. Not so Aron. He tucked into the mountainous pile of sandwiches that their grandmother made as if he hadn't eaten for a week. Afterwards, they helped to clear up and then went to watch television. Mistaking their weary expressions for tiredness and unaccustomed fresh air, Neve announced an early night for them all. "Teeth, toilet, turn out the lights and sleep. Okay?"

"Okay" They replied in unison, not minding a bit.

Before getting into bed Larna removed the GPS from under her pillow and placed it inside her jacket pocket ready for tomorrow, just in case they had an opportunity to use it. As she hunkered down in her comfortable bed, she thought of the young man she'd seen in her dream the previous night and wondered if she'd have any more strange dreams. Maybe they would answer some of the questions still swirling round in her head. With this happy thought, she nodded off.

"BOO!"

Larna jumped big time in her dream. Then a voice said, "So sorry, Larna, didn't mean to startle you."

"Who *are* you?" At first, Larna couldn't see a thing, only a dark swirling mist. "*Where* are you?"

"The answer to your questions will only make sense when you are actually here," the voice answered, beginning to morph into the shape of the boy she had seen so many times in her dreams.

"What do you mean by 'here'?"

"It will all make sense in due course," the boy repeated.

"I hope so... " began Larna, but then everything in front of her began to disappear, gradually fading out of sight. She could hear the young man calling her name as he faded away. The shock of it woke her up. On opening her eyes, her grandmother was standing at the side of the bed, looking down at her with a strange expression.

"Are you alright, Larna?" she whispered. "I heard you talking in your sleep."

"Yeah, I think so. I had a weird dream." Yaya's cool hand touched her forehead. "It was so real."

"Yes love, it would be," replied her grandmother, as if she knew what she had dreamt.

Larna could feel herself drifting back to sleep and just managed to say, "g'night before Neve left, leaving the door partly open so that the landing light shone dimly through.

"Good night, safe dreams," she called.

Within a matter of moments, Larna started dreaming again and found herself taking the same course as before. But, just as she was about to meet the strange young man again, she was faced with a brick wall – a high, solid brick wall – which she could neither get over or around. Try as she might, she just could not get to the other side, so she decided she'd had enough and gave up. She felt very upset about this, deeply unhappy that the path to her friend had been blocked by someone or something. So she sat by the wall and waited, but nobody came. She felt alone and friendless in a strange world, the same sense of approaching doom that she'd felt in the garden that afternoon seeping into her bones.

Larna woke to the sound of a very noisy bird on her windowsill. Checking the watch still on her wrist, she realised she'd woken up before the alarm was due to go off at 7.30 a.m. Neve's head popped round the door.

"Morning, Larna! Sleep well after that little hiccup in the night?" She smiled brightly.

"Like a log actually."

"Aron's still asleep, but you could come down and have breakfast with me in the kitchen."

"Sounds good to me. Be down shortly."

Larna was just eating her cereal when Aron entered the kitchen still only half-awake but already dressed in jeans and top. He headed straight for the food and plonked himself down opposite Larna.

"Morning, sleep well?" Larna asked smugly, knowing he didn't appreciate polite conversation first thing in the morning.

Aron scowled at his sister. "Yeah, fine."

Then Neve hurried out of the room to answer the telephone.

"I had that dream again last night," Larna whispered.

"So?" Aron shrugged grumpily.

Larna felt annoyed at his lack of interest. She felt her dreams were a key to the mystery. But she just shrugged and said, "Oh well, if you're not bothered. Still on for some more geocaching?"

Aron perked up at this, his mouth full of cereal. "Yeah that's what we'd planned, isn't it?"

Larna grinned. That was more like it!

It wasn't long before Neve came back into the kitchen, smiling. "Guess what? I've just been invited to be guest speaker at the church hall this morning. The speaker they booked has been taken ill and they've asked me to be a last-minute replacement. Will you two be alright for a couple of hours on your own?"

They nodded vigorously.

"What will you do while I'm gone?"

Thinking quickly on her feet, Larna said, "We haven't given it much thought, Yaya. I expect we'll do the same as yesterday."

"As you wish, but with the same proviso. Now then, what shall I speak about? I know! It'll have to be my favourite subject. Nature's own medicines. Plants that possess healing powers."

"In that case, why do we need doctors?" queried Aron.

"I haven't time to discuss this now, dear," said their grandmother, sorting out some books containing large coloured pictures of wild plants that she intended to use to illustrate her talk. Then she wandered off to make some notes, leaving Larna and Aron alone. They looked at each other, nodded and made a dash for the door. Neither wanted to waste a moment of their precious freedom. But Neve stopped them in their tracks.

"Hang on a minute," she called. "Why don't you come with me? You might learn something."

They felt their blood run cold.

"We'll be fine on our own, Yaya, honestly." Aron said quickly.

"Okay. On second thoughts, there'll be a lot of sitting around and you'd probably be bored stiff. So you do your own thing. Just remember, if you do go into the woods, no further than the big tree. Okay?"

Suddenly, Larna remembered something, "I need to go upstairs and get the GPS," she whispered to Aron. "Cover for me, okay?"

So while Aron pretended to be interested in Neve's illustrations, Larna dashed upstairs, collected the GPS and the clues and key-ring and was back downstairs in sixty seconds flat. She gave her grandmother a glancing peck on the cheek, still on the move, and grabbed Aron by his jacket. Together they raced outside and shouted, "Bye! See you later." If there was a reply, they didn't stop to hear it. They headed straight for the garden gate.

A voice on the breeze... "Remember the rules. Always stick together. Have fun."

They came to an abrupt halt, turned and saw the sprightly old lady making her way to the garage, handbag in one hand, swinging her car keys in the other.

"Why does she keep saying that, stick together?" Aron snorted.

"Dunno. Daresay she means well." Larna shrugged.

CHAPTER SIX

Aron pushed the gate open and held it as Larna's hands were full, holding the GPS and clues. They headed deeper into the forest. With an occasional glance backwards, they heaved a sigh of relief as they heard the roar of the MG's engine and the spitting of gravel as their grandmother sped away.

With co-ordinates in the GPS, they found they were being directed beyond the big tree again, then to the area where they needed the clues. This time neither of them gave a second thought about breaking their promise.

There seemed to be a lot more wildlife than yesterday. Trees were full of birds all competing to be heard. For a few seconds Aron and Larna were the quietest they'd been in a long time.

"I see you're back then." said a disembodied voice.

They looked around. Nothing.

"Okay" Larna replied, exasperated. The calm and quiet mood was broken. She glanced up into the trees. "Whoever you are, show yourself."

"Be careful where you put your feet. I'm down here."
The large black crow from yesterday peered up at them from its stance at their feet.

"It *is* you. You're actually speaking to us!" The absurdity of it brought about the onset of fits of nervous laughter. "I'm talking to a bird!" Pausing to inhale, Larna wiped her eyes and looked around. The air stilled. Everything seemed to be holding its collective breath. Then the hairs on her neck started to prickle.
Slowly, before their eyes, the bird began to change. Firstly the legs, now clad in green, lengthened into human form. Then the body grew to about Aron's height filling out a long black mac. The wings extended until they filled the sleeves and bony fingers crept out

of the ends. In fear Larna and Aron scrambled backwards, but unable to look away they sat on a rock and watched the final part of the transformation take place. A shock of unruly red hair topped a narrow face with two fangs protruding from the corners of the mouth. Penetrating blue eyes looked back at them from under bushy red eyebrows.

Still in shock Aron gasped, "Clem, is that you? What's going on? Where's the bird gone?"

Bending down, Clem grabbed the youngsters and hauled them up. "There's no need to be afraid, you two. I know it's very confusing for you at the moment. There are many things you do not know or understand yet. But soon you will. I am here to guide you on your journey, don't ya know."

"What journey are you talking about? We aren't going anywhere. We've already gone further than we promised. Yaya'll have a fit if she finds out." Aron was beginning to take things more seriously now.

"I know all that. But I'm also sure that in these exceptional circumstances your grandmother would fully understand. Stand next to the cache and nature will form a circle round you. That's when your journey begins."

Ordinarily Aron was the sceptic while Larna had blind faith, but this time she was the one to challenge Clem. "How are we going to travel?" she said, snapping her fingers in the air. "By magic?"

At that precise moment a piece of paper drifted down and landed at her feet. Bending to pick it up Larna realised it was the note to them from the cache box they'd found yesterday. Clem nodded to the paper in her hand. "Now, if you're ready... ?" Aron squeezed his sister's shoulder and Larna automatically did the same to him. Each realised the other was scared stiff but trying not to show it.

"There's no need to feel afraid. You have many friends where you are going." The old man paused. "I promise you'll receive an explanation at the other end. Larna, you've already been to the other side in your dreams, though somewhat briefly I know. They wanted to make initial contact with you whilst you slept."

Larna and Aron looked at each other, unsure whether to go on or go back.

"If you follow the instructions to the letter," continued Clem invitingly. "I promise your spirit of adventure won't be disappointed."

"Shall we go for it?" Larna asked Aron.

"Yes, I think we should. But don't ask me why."

"Okay, we'll do it, Clem. But will you stay with us?"

"I wish I could, but sadly I'm unable to. My place is here to protect the contents of the cache box, but there will be someone to meet you at the other end." He leaned his head to one side. "A piece of advice you must always obey. Whatever happens, *stay together* and you will be fine."

With his bony left hand he motioned them towards the cache, now partly visible in front of him. Suddenly the morning sun came out from behind a cloud and a shaft of golden light shone down onto the lid of the box. "When you're ready, read the final instructions."

Nervously, Larna picked up the note and read it out loud for Aron's benefit...

Larna, being the eldest in line, must remove the key from the box. Aron, the second offspring, must say 'Ella Vita' three time. A monolith will rise from the

earth in the shape of a door. Use the key and then step through.

"Ready?" Clem asked, holding his hand out for the note. "You can't take this with you."

After handing it over, Larna and Aron stepped forwards and Clem stepped back. Suddenly leaves began to swirl up. Then they dropped back to the ground, having formed a large circle round them. Larna looked at the old man and saw he was pointing urgently at the cache box, reminding her to pick up the key. Glancing at Aron, Larna double-checked he was still happy to go ahead. He nodded and gave her a thumbs-up sign. So, drawing a deep breath, Larna bent down and opened the box and was surprised to see the key back in place, but in a better condition. She picked it up in her right hand. Then Clem motioned to Aron to begin. Anxiously clearing his throat he began, *"ELLA VITA, ELLA VITA, ELLA VITA."*

There was a rumbling sound beneath them and the ground started to shake. On the edge of the circle, a large block of stone slowly pushed its way through the earth until it reached Larna's height and stopped. Totally overawed, she couldn't fathom where the key was to go. Turning her head towards Clem for help, she saw he was pointing a long finger in the direction of the stone and was just in time to see a red glow appear within the rock. In a matter of seconds it had burnt a hole large enough for the key. It was obvious what she was supposed to do next. Holding onto Aron, she stepped forwards and, with a shaky hand, managed to insert the key and turn it.

CHAPTER SEVEN

The heavy stone slab quietly opened away from them creating a passageway, the key still in place. A sudden rush of warm air enveloped them for just a brief moment. Larna felt no fear, but nevertheless was compelled to shut her eyes as they stepped through the portal together.

"You can open your eyes now," said a softly spoken voice that Larna recognised from somewhere within her memory. She did as she was asked and the first thing she saw was a carpet of flowers, red bells instead of blue.

"You okay?" she asked her brother anxiously.

Running his hands down his body in an exaggerated check he answered, "Yeah. Where are we?"

"I'm relieved to see you arrived in one piece," the soft voice said again. Larna turned, facing the same direction as Aron, and found the boy standing in front of them, hands on hips, big grin on his face. The boy from her dreams. She was struck by the intense green of his big almond-shaped eyes and his dog-like nose. Instead of the colourful outfit he'd worn before, he was wearing a gothic-style black coat which nearly touched the ground, and their ruby key was sticking out of his top pocket.

"Unbelievable!" was all Larna could stutter. Aron was similarly afflicted.

"Hi Larna, it's so good to meet you in the flesh at last. You do recognise me, don't you?"

"Of course I do," croaked Larna. "You haunt my sleep."

"I'm sorry about that, but I needed to contact you and the only way I could do so in your world was via your dreams."

"So you weren't telling porkies," murmured Aron.

Larna gave her brother a brief smile and then turned to the boy.

"Who are you?" she asked.

He gave a mock bow and smiled at them. "My name is Tiblou, but you can call me Tibs for short. Everyone else does."

"Can you tell us where we are, Tibs? Am I still dreaming?"

"No you're not, Larna, you're in the same place but in another time... "

Before he could explain any further, a large velvety black crow appeared between them.

"Clem! I thought you said you couldn't travel with us," exclaimed Aron.

"I'm *not* Clem. I'm *Clementine*, his twin sister," she said crossly. "He is the guardian of the key to the porthole in your time. I am the guardian in this time."

"What do you mean, 'in this time'?" asked Larna.

"All I am at liberty to say right now is that you aren't in the twenty-first century anymore."

Tiblou and Clementine glanced at each other and exchanged a knowing look. Then, like Clem had done, the bird began to change into human-like form becoming the feminine version of Clem. The only difference was that she had masses of long carroty red hair which was completely wild, as if it hadn't been brushed for years. Her predominantly green clothes were flamboyant and flowing.

Tiblou looked back and noticed his visitors looking anxious and confused. "Everything will be explained very shortly, but right now I need to escort you to my home because it looks like we're about to have the daily downpour."

"Daily?" Aron queried.

"Every single day." Tiblou wrinkled his brows. "Why, doesn't it do that in your time?"

"Where we live, you just never know when it's going to rain," replied Larna. Thinking of home made her shiver.

Clementine disappeared as they began to follow Tiblou. The sky was beginning to get dark, the clouds heavy with rain.

"Come on, you two. Pick up some speed !"

Soon they were practically running through the forest. Larna noticed movement out of the corner of her eye. Still on the trot, she glanced to her right, but whatever it was had vanished. She shrugged it off as her imagination running wild. But again she caught sight of movement, this time at the other side. Arriving at Tiblou's house she turned as fast as she could in an attempt to catch who or whatever it was she thought she'd seen. But still there was nothing. Whatever it was could move, and move fast.

"What's wrong?" asked Tiblou.

"I don't know. I had the strangest feeling we were being followed. But every time I looked round, there was nothing there." Tiblou looked very worried, but gave a reassuring smile. "There is a possibility we were being watched, but it's nothing for you to worry about."

The casual way he said it didn't make Larna feel any easier. "Okay, Tibs, I'll take your word for it," she said reluctantly. A further glance around proved there was no one there. Nevertheless it didn't stop Larna feeling uncomfortable. Aron, of course, seemed oblivious.

CHAPTER EIGHT

L egs aching and out of breath, Larna stood and gazed in wonder at Tiblou's house. It was shaped like a dome with a mass of unusual plants of every description surrounding it. It had two visible windows that were huge and looked strange, positioned either side of a very small door. Tibs had dashed ahead and was unlocking this. He stood aside to let them in just as the heavens opened and the first drops of rain descended on their heads. Aron and Larna leapt inside to avoid getting soaked. Then they watched from the safety of Tiblou's window as the rain bounced waist high. They'd never seen rain like it.

Making his way to the centre of the room, Tiblou turned to welcome them with a smile on his face. The room they found themselves in was the sitting area. Not terribly large and with a pleasant shade of light green covering the walls and crystal vases full of exotic looking flowers sat on both windowsills. Furniture was sparse. Two yellow armchairs and two dining table chairs with animal carvings all over them. And a coffee table with similar markings to the chairs. To the left, was a medium-sized fireplace made from a light tan marble, not unlike their one at home.

The rain clouds caused the room to be suddenly filled with weird dark shadows. Tiblou switched on the lights, instantly banishing the gloom and lightening the mood. Indicating to the chairs, he said, "Sit down and get your breath back." They walked towards an equally small door on the opposite wall and said, "I need a drink. What about you?"

"Yes, please!" they said together.

Moments later, Tiblou re-entered carrying a green triangular tray supporting three cups. Their design was unusual. They looked like three balls with colourful straws peeking out of the top. Aron took a huge slug. "Apple juice!" He continued to slurp away happily. Larna drew the liquid up the straw, savouring the taste on her tongue, then licked her lips. It was fantastic. "Mine's orange!" she exclaimed. "No bits either. It's delicious. I don't think I've ever tasted fruit juice as good as this." She looked quizzically at Tiblou. "How did you know what we liked. We never told you."

"The cups do all the work," he explained. "They sense what you'd like as soon as you grasp them. So everybody always gets what they want."

"Awesome," said Aron. "How does it work?"

"I've no idea, just does. Drink up and enjoy it."

Tiblou removed his long coat. Larna gasped as a tail unfurled. Shakily putting her cup down on the coffee table, she rubbed her eyes in disbelief and then had another look to double-check. She coughed quietly to attract Aron's attention. He was miles away in awe of his magic juice, so it took several seconds before his mouth also opened in astonishment.

"I wondered how long it would take you to notice my tail," chuckled Tibs. He was obviously amused by their reaction.

"Where did it come from?" asked Aron, never one to hold back.

"It's a long story," sighed Tiblou, suddenly becoming serious. "That is why you two have been brought here. We need your help."

"*Our* help?" queried Larna, making a puzzled face at Aron. "What have we got to do with anything?"

"And who exactly is 'we'?" Aron added.

"I'll explain," said Tiblou. Taking a deep breath, he began to tell them a horrendous tale.

* * *

"When you stepped through that portal, the one guarded by Clem and Clementine, you travelled through time into the future." he began. "You are now many years ahead of the twenty-first century. The gap between our time and yours is large and filled with all your descendants. Two of your great-great-great grandchildren – I can't remember how many generations exactly, but it was a lot – were brilliant scientists. They were cousins by the name of

Pamela and Andrew and they worked in medicine. Neurology, the study of the brain and nervous system, was their speciality... and their passion. They had a relative, someone very dear to them, who had a serious neurological disease for which they were determined to find a cure – or, at least, a way to keep them in permanent remission. Up until then, most people who suffered from this disease ended up in wheelchairs. But thanks to Pamela and Andrew's brilliant research, all this suffering was consigned to the history books."

"Unfortunately, there was a down-side to their success. One of their colleagues, an eminent professor called Kristoff Sharpe, became insanely jealous and wanted to destroy them. He began by stealing their notes and passing them off as his own, but when this was exposed, he tried setting fire to their research. Fortunately, the laboratory sprinklers kicked in and most of it was saved. But Sharpe wasn't finished yet. One day, he gained access to the lab and contaminated the precious serum used to treat the illness with several different types of animal D.N.A. He hoped this would cause worldwide devastation and discredit Pamela and Andrew completely. He was caught soon afterwards and the two scientists were seen to be innocent of any wrong-doing. But it was too late. The contaminated serum had been distributed and many people had taken it. The results for them and their descendants were catastrophic... "

He indicated his tail. Then he shrugged dramatically and spread his arms. "And that is why we are living within in this dome, beautiful as it is... "

* * *

Tiblou's dramatic story was interrupted by a double knock on the door. All of them jumped, wondering who or what might be on the other side. Tiblou tutted, stood up and headed across the room. He squinted through a tiny spy hole, nodded to himself and quickly opened the door to admit a smartly dressed, petite-looking lady with short wavy brown hair. She was about five feet two and with the same deformities as Tibs, – a dog-like nose and a long tail. She stood just inside the room clutching a handbag tightly with both hands. The huge smile on her face put Larna and Aron at ease straight away.

Giving Tiblou a peck on the cheek she said fondly, "Good morning dear. It's stopped raining so I thought I'd pay you a visit." She lowered her voice and said conspiratorially, "I've brought some of your favourite choc-chip-spirals. I baked them specially this morning."

"Thanks, ma." He turned to face Larna and Aron, "I'd like you to meet my mother Annie." He stepped aside. They stared at Annie and she smiled at them. They were at a loss for words, so Annie took the initiative and enveloped them in a fragrant hug.

"Oh, I'm thrilled to meet you two. It's so exciting that this day has finally come. I hope our appearance doesn't scare you."

"Not now."

Aron chipped in, "Speak for yourself, sis. I'm still getting used to it."

Annie looked across at her son. "Have you told them everything, dear?"

"I was in the middle of it, mum, when you knocked... "

"Well, you'd better get on with it then, hadn't you?" She smiled lovingly at Tibs and made herself comfortable on one of the dining chairs.

"Where was I?" he wondered, scratching his head.

"You were talking about a dome," Aron prompted him.

"Oh, yes. The dome. When it became apparent that so many people had been affected, the ones who weren't afflicted were scared for themselves and their children and persuaded the World Governments to build this bubble. It has its own life-support system and anyone showing signs of being infected is immediately moved inside, allegedly to save the rest of humanity. People outside can't see in and conversely we can't look out. By the miracles of modern technology, we *can* see the moon, feel the heat of the sun and experience all the seasons just like the outsiders. We have everything we need. We're imprisoned here, but it's not a bad life really, is it mum?"

"No, love, it's not. At least until now."

Larna and Aron wondered what Annie meant by that, but they were interrupted by another knock on the door. This time Annie called out to the unseen visitor.

"Hello dear, come on in."

A head with shoulder-length brown hair peeped in with a cheeky smile for them all. Larna instantly knew he was related to Annie and Tibs. Same colouring, same bearing. He crossed the room, bent down and gave her a quick kiss on the forehead. Then he stood next to Tiblou and Larna noticed he was a good three inches taller than their friend.

"Before you ask, mum, I'm fine. You?"

"Oh very excited, dear." She nodded in their guests' direction. "As you can see, Larna and Aron have arrived. Can you believe it? They're finally here... "

Again, the two of them didn't understand how Annie knew they were coming or what their role was in all of this, but it wasn't the time to ask.

"Before we go any further," boomed the newcomer, "I think introductions are necessary, don't you?" He turned to the visitors and held out his hand. "Hi, my name's Chet. I'm Tiblou's older brother, by two years."

They shook hands, Chet's being firm and steady. Then he asked, "Has my brother filled you in?"

"He's told us about the mutant D.N.A. and the dome," answered Aron.

"About half then," said Chet.

"And the rest will have to wait until a little bit later," Annie cut in. "We're being very rude to our young guests. You two must be starving... "

"We are pretty hungry," agreed Larna, knowing she spoke for Aron even more than herself. "It seems forever since we last had something to eat."

"That settles it!" exclaimed Annie, turning to Tibou. "You take Larna and Aron for some food. I'll stay here with Chet. Afterwards, you can finish explaining the terrifying situation we find ourselves in. I'm sure our young friends here will take it in much better when their stomachs are full."

CHAPTER NINE

Tiblou tucked his arms through Larna and Aron's and led them away from the house. "I'll take you to Uncle Roger's Kitchen Café for the best home cooking. Uncle Roger is mum's brother. They're very close."

As they walked along Larna felt a cold shiver down her spine and a feeling of apprehension. They were definitely being watched again. Suddenly her vision blurred and dark shadows moved within the hidden depths of the trees. She gasped in terror.

"Come on, you two," urged Tibs, pulling them along in a power walk. Larna wasn't sure whether she'd sensed something too or was just in a hurry to eat.When Larna looked round again, everything had returned to normal.

From the amazing smells wafting through the air, she knew they weren't very far from the café. Larna smiled as she saw Tiblou's nose twitching and making loud sniffing noises as animals do – or, in his case, part-animal. The café was well lit and very colourful. The roof was red and the walls were yellow. It looked a fun place to eat. As they entered, the chatter stopped abruptly. Everybody turned to look at them and Larna noticed they all had tails, though many were of different animal species. One woman had what appeared to be a cat's tail, black with a white tip. Another had a swishing horse's tail... and so on. There were so many different forms of mutation, although Larna noticed that the parents and children of each family looked the same.

They sat down and Tiblou's uncle brought the menu in person. He also had canine ears, nose and the good long tail, like a more advanced version of Tibs. Roger was roughly Chet's height, his hair short and grey and his eyes large and green. He looked smart with the name of his cafe printed in black on the front of his yellow uniform. He gave them a huge smile then held out his arm in greeting.

"You are most welcome," he said, handing out some menus. "Now what would you like to eat?"

Larna chose multi-coloured rice with chicken in a thick purple sauce. Aron found it hard to decide, but eventually opted for the green cheese pasta because he liked the picture of it on the menu. And Tibs asked for his usual, blue pastry pie with speedy sauce. The food was delicious – literally out of this world – and tasted like nothing Larna and Aron had ever experienced before. It was followed by some mouth-watering desserts that grew on trees in the back garden, like Christmas trees with edible presents. They went outside to choose what they wanted. By the time they'd gone back for seconds... and thirds... Larna and Aron felt uncomfortably full.

"I won't need to eat again for a week," groaned Aron, patting his distended stomach.

"Yeah, right," scoffed Larna, knowing her brother voracious appetite.

When the meal was over, the other diners picked up their chairs and formed a circle around the visitors' table. Annie and Chet also arrived, looking very sombre. They sat either side of Roger who made room for them in silence. Then everyone turned expectantly to Tiblou, waiting for him to speak. The mood had turned serious and Larna realised they were finally about to learn the terrible danger that faced these good people.

* * *

Tibs stood in front of his audience, but he didn't say a word. Instead, to Larna and Aron's horror and amazement, his features began to change! His outline started to shimmer, and within seconds, they were staring at a completely different person standing next to Tibs. The newcomer looked much older than Tiblou. He had a waist-length blue beard and matching long straight hair, partially hiding a pair of large twinkling blue eyes. A long and predominantly blue multi-coloured robe completed his outfit. Larna and Aron were gob-smacked. They just stared.

Amused by their response, the strange man opened his mouth and spoke.

"I bet you weren't expecting that," he chuckled.

They couldn't speak.

"I see you are tongue-tied," he continued, "so I'll start the ball rolling myself. My name is Balgaire. I am what you call a wizard – a good one, I hasten to add."

Still no response from Larna or Aron.

"As you see, I have powers which enable me to materialise through other people." He laughed self-consciously. "It beats having to walk here. Saves time!"

"Why are we here, Balgaire?" asked Larna, finding her voice at last and coming straight to the point.

Balgaire indicated the audience with a wide sweep of his arm.

"We need your help to stop this mutation becoming more prevalent," he explained. "The poison in their bodies has begun to mutate again. If it's not reversed, everyone here will eventually change completely into the animal whose dominant DNA was in the system of their forbears. For example, Tiblou's family will revert to being wolves. Many have already gone through this transition already. It's heart-breaking."

"I still don't see where we fit into all this," put in Aron. "How can we, a couple of school kids from the past, possibly help you?"

"We need to take a little blood from you both," explained the wizard. "Because of your bloodline, your family history that goes right back through Pamela and Andrew and beyond, you're not contaminated. So we need to access your pure D.N.A. to produce a new serum that will halt and hopefully reverse all these horrific mutations."

Larna felt a huge wave of relief flooding through her. It wouldn't be a problem to give blood. Strictly speaking, they weren't old enough to do so, but this was a dire emergency and it would only be the once. It wouldn't take long, either. They could do their good deed and go back to their own time, something she longed to do and knew Aron did too. But her elation was only momentary. Her spirits sank again as Balgaire told them about the evil force behind the new mutations.

"The speeding-up of these mutations, which have been stable for hundreds of years, is the work of a warlock called Mordrog. He was a pupil of mine when he was young, a brilliant student who learned everything I taught him with effortless ease, but when he grew up he turned to the dark side and started using his new-found powers for personal gain. Now we are deadly enemies. He intends to destroy me and I intend to stop his evil plan.

"And what is that?" asked Aron.

"When the mutations are complete, our people become animals with a human brain and the power of speech. They are highly sought-after in the outside world where they are used by the military. They are used for spying or are thrust into your endless conflicts and many get injured or slaughtered. But, if Mordrog has his way, there'll be a steady supply of them in the future. Each one commands a huge price and he'll be rich beyond his wildest dreams before long, money he can invest in further evil deeds. And nobody knows anything about this business except the poor souls whom he enslaves. The whole thing is kept top secret by the military."

"So it's not just a case of giving blood and going home," murmured Larna, speaking her thoughts out loud.

"Mordrog will do everything in his power – which is awesome – to stop us reversing these mutations," sighed Balgaire. "So it's no use your giving your blood until it's safe to do so. Mordrog has to be defeated before anything can be changed."

Larna looked at the sea of worried faces surrounding her and something surged within her. She couldn't leave these kind people to their fate. She glanced at her brother who was thinking exactly the same. He gave her a nod. So she turned to their new friends with a brave smile.

"We'll stay and help in the fight," she said.

CHAPTER TEN

O utside the café, the leaves on the ground began to swirl about and then started hammering on the door and windows as if sounding a warning. Fear clutched everyone's heart and, before anyone could stop them, Larna and Aron got up and walked to the door. Some force was drawing them outside as if by an invisible string. Knowing what this must be, Balgaire hurried after them, anxious for their safety. The three of them stood amidst the dancing leaves until a menacing figure materialised in front of them. Larna knew immediately it must be Mordrog. He was over six feet tall with greasy black shoulder-length hair. His eyes were amber with a rim of red, as if he'd been awake for years. The rest of him was hidden beneath a swathe of jet-black clothing, from neck to toe. His stare was menacing as if emitting waves of evil. Larna and Aron felt terrified.

Uncle Roger appeared in the doorway behind them, spreading his arms to hold back everyone who had followed him out of the café. He was the first to speak.

"What do *you* want?" he demanded contemptuously.

Mordrog put his hands on his hips and sneered, "I heard you had a couple of guests. It would be very churlish of me not to welcome them personally, don't you think?" Then he leaned forwards in an aggressive manner. "What have you been telling these young people?"

Roger took a couple of steps forwards to face him, the other diners pressing their backs against the café wall in obvious fear of the confrontation.

"You have no business with our visitors and you are certainly *not* welcome here." said Roger defiantly.

Larna found herself literally rooted to the spot, unable to move her legs. But she found her voice. "You're Mordrog, aren't you?" The warlock turned to look at her. "So," he said, inclining his head, "I see I *have* been mentioned already." He leaned towards Larna who tried to back away but couldn't. Instead, she lost her balance and finished in a squat, looking up into amber eyes which seemed to peer deep inside her head.

"Stay away from her!" yelled Roger.

Balgaire began to laugh. A high-pitched cackle, cruel. Aron tried to move closer to help his sister but found he was also stuck to the spot. They were both petrified. Then Mordrog turned to Roger, breaking eye-contact with Larna, who gave a huge sigh of relief and pulled herself upright again.

"I sense that you are about to threaten me, in front of witnesses, and these nice young people." He laughed again. "Am I supposed to quiver in my shoes and run away?"

"I wish you would," snarled Roger. "You've caused enough pain and suffering here, so don't even think of involving them in your evil plans."

"You *are* threatening me! What evil plans?"

"You know perfectly well what I'm talking about. You have dispatched so many of our friends to the other side, condemning them to perpetual slavery, humiliation and despair at the mercy of corrupt moguls of industry and war mongers."

Mordrog threw his head back and laughed, then just as abruptly became serious. "You should be very happy," he muttered. "At least they are still alive."

Uncle Roger quivered with rage and raised his fist. For a minute Larna thought he was going to deliver a hefty blow to Modrog's chin, but Balgaire stepped forwards just in time. "What do you want?" he asked with a weary sigh.

"I thought it was time to introduce myself to our visitors. And there is another side to my business which no doubt differs from whatever you've filled their heads with. They might even favour my version above yours and refuse to help you."

Chet appeared and pushed his way to the front. "You are unbelievably conceited if you think anyone would trust a thing you say."

Modrog spun round and glared with such intensity that Chet began to shake. "Nobody asked you," he sneered and increased the power of his gaze causing Chet to double up with pain and crumple to the ground, head in his hands.

"Why are you doing this?" Aron yelled. "You should be ashamed of yourself!"

Larna felt overwhelming pride for her brother and would have hugged him if she'd been able to move.

"What lies have you been told?" demanded the warlock. "I help these creatures to find their destiny. They aren't sad, I give you my word." He held out his right arm to shake Aron's hand. Larna's brother responded by shoving his hands deep into his trouser pockets.

Prompted by her brother's courageous outburst, Larna felt she had to make a stand too. "I don't believe a word of what you are saying. They must be suffering. In fact, I think you enjoy making them suffer. You must have made your millions by now, so why don't you leave the rest of them alone?"

"I don't like your tone, Larna. There's no need to be so critical. I consider these people as friends, that's why I help them move on." He tapped his chest. "You must think I have an empty space in here, but I don't. I have a heart, a rather large one as it happens."

Larna could feel herself being drawn towards him. He was exerting some kind of mental power over her and everything else was becoming distant and quiet. It was just the two of them facing each other, eyes locked. Then the tension was broken by a strange surprise.

Something moved in one of Balgaire's vast pockets, working its way up, trying to squeeze itself out. It emerged, coughing and spluttering; a four inch... something... that began to grow to about eight inches. Larna realised it must be a type of fairy. Obviously female, wearing a long, black, lacy dress with three-quarter sleeves showing tiny wrists and hands, with three fingers and something at the side resembling a thumb.. Her feet were hidden. She unfurled translucent, rainbow-coloured wings which, as they stretched and fluttered, began to darken until they matched her dress. Her delicate features were neither beautiful nor ugly, just unusual. Her eyes were coal black, like her full lips. Masses of long wavy bright purple hair framed her face, the only relief from the black. The Goth-like creature in front of them seemed to possess a gentleness that was appealing. She flew up and hovered in mid-air by Balgaire's left shoulder. Larna longed to know who she was, but it wasn't the time to ask. With a smile, Balgaire turned back to Mordrog. "You were saying?"

The warlock recovered his composure, but did not look back at Larna. Her vision suddenly returned and so did the background noises. She realised he had been hypnotising her... and succeeding. Sensing he was getting nowhere, Mordrog tried another tack. His voice became coaxing.

"Why don't you join me?" he said to Larna and Aron. "I can make you unbelievably rich! Imagine... " he waved the air as if conjuring up pictures of his promises... "you would be able to buy anything your heart desired." He paused to let his words sink in. "Dream it and you will have it. Ask me and I will make it happen. All you have to do is come over to my side... "

Balgaire spoke up, "I credit these youngsters with more sense than to fall for that drivel. It appears you've had a wasted journey."

"I see the puppet-master speaks for his little friends! Come on, you two, can't you speak for yourselves? When you are older you will have huge dreams which can only be fulfilled with a bottomless purse." He started to concentrate more on Aron, sensing he may be more susceptible to the prospect of an easy life. "Just think what you could buy for yourselves."

Everyone's eyes were on them now. Larna's legs were beginning to turn to jelly and she wasn't certain how long she could remain upright under such pressure. Aron, too, felt very distressed. The warlock's overpowering will was making them waver. Annie sensed this and intervened.

"Oh *do* shut up. Mordrog! You heard them. They're not going to take any notice of you or listen to your nonsense."

He looked down on Annie with disgust. "Your progeny have inherited your bad manners, madam, and your recklessness. Why do you persist in meddling in my affairs, especially when you know that all will suffer the consequences from your interference?"

Mordrog's eyes started to turn red from the rims inward again as he sought out Larna and Aron. Still anchored to the ground, they felt the twin beams boring into their minds. Both their hearts began to race, their eyes rolled up, as the warlock slowly sapped their resistance. Then, suddenly, Annie rushed forward, both arms outstretched, and with an angry cry, gave Mordrog an almighty shove. Taken completely by surprise, he lost his balance and sprawled on the ground in an ungainly manner. The hypnotic rays wavered and faded and the freed pair found they could move again. Everyone looked shocked and fearfully drew back. But Balgaire stepped forward to banish the villain.

"Return to the black hole you came from," he ordered. "We never want to see you're vile face again."

Mordrog knew he'd failed to win Larna and Aron over. So, once again, the leaves rose from the ground and formed a circle above the warlock's head. They began to spin. The force dragged in more twigs and small stones from further afield like a giant vacuum. The circle grew tighter and tighter around Mordrog so all that could be seen was a look of hatred and fury on his face before he disappeared.

"You will pay for this!" he snarled.

* * *

As the leaves settled down again, a strange smell reached Larna's nose, making her head reel. It was an exhilarating smell, full of life and power.

"Where did Mordrog go?" Aron wanted to know.

"We... " Balgaire pointing to his little friend, "have sent him back to the Dark Side using our combined strength and the potency of the leaves. I'm sure you can smell the cleanness of the air now." He wiped his brow on the back of his sleeve. "But, he will be back, that is a certainty, and the battle will begin in earnest."

This was a terrifying prospect. In an attempt to change the subject Larna asked, "Who is your friend, Balgaire? She's awesome!"

The aura round the tiny being began to glow and the translucent wings to flutter whilst emitting wonderful colours which seemed to float in the air then slowly disappear like star dust. It was breath-taking. She flew over to Balgaire and whispered in his ear. Larna heard the gentle sound of her laughter. Then she flew to her and she felt the fairy's soft touch on her cheek, gentle kiss of air that made the teenager catch her breath in wonder.

"Her name is Violet," said Balgaire. "My little miracle-worker stays close to me, sensing when I'm in danger and need her most." He smiled again. Unfortunately, she's the last of her kind which makes her unique. Extra special."

By now, the diners had gradually drifted back inside the Kitchen Café and were starting to go home. Balgaire spoke softly to Violet, thanking her for her help before bidding her farewell. Until the next crisis, no doubt. In a flash she disappeared. This left Balgaire, Tiblou, Chet, Annie, Aron and Larna wondering what to do next.

The wizard raised his arms to the sky, closed his eyes and mumbled something unintelligible. The leaves that had encircled Mordrog slowly drifted towards Balgaire and, in slow motion, began to circle him. More and more gathered speed until he could no longer be seen. The perfume from the flying leaves was heady and strong. Larna stepped back and nearly fell. Aron steadied her. What was happening now? A faint amber glow from within the mini-whirlwind emitted rays which spun like a dizzy top. As suddenly as it began it slowed, gently scattering the leaves which fluttered to the ground, leaving Balgaire swaying slightly and breathless. For a few seconds he just stood there, in front of the youngsters, looking spaced-out. The amber light seemed to glow then fade, rhythmically, as if beating in time to his heart. Aron and Larna glanced at the others. They didn't seem to find this unusual at all. As the pulsing light began to dim, Balgaire shook his head several times and seemed to return to his normal self.

"I have taken a glimpse into the future," he explained, "and what I have seen is very worrying. We must leave here at once. Otherwise it will be too late!"

"Too late for what?" queried Larna.

"Too late for you to give your blood. Mordrog will do everything in his power to stop that happening."

Balgaire beckoned everyone to follow him. As they hurried away from the café, they turned and waved goodbye to Uncle Roger.

"Good luck, you two. Hope to see you again soon," he called.

"Come along, *please,* before it's too late." The urgency in Balgaire's voice abruptly ended the farewell.

The scent from the leaves wasn't quite as strong and the fragrance now had a soothing effect on the senses. Aron looked remarkably calm under the circumstances. Suddenly realising her brother wasn't scared anymore, Larna laughed out loud, then self-consciously clapped her free hand over her mouth. Aron grinned at her and winked.

They rushed right past Tiblou's house and, for a split second, Larna thought they were going to get lost. Lagging a bit behind Balgaire and Tibs, but ahead of Annie and Chet by a couple of paces, she wondered where they were being taken. Hurrying deeper into the woods she noticed the leaves had lost their heady perfume altogether and that's when the feeling of euphoria began to wane. As she tried to analyse her changing emotions, Larna had a strong feeling that they were being watched again. Turning her head, she thought she saw movement in the trees. She looked again. Nothing. But as she hurried to catch up with the others, she glanced back quickly and caught sight of a pair of angry greeny-yellow eyes peeping from behind a large tree. Watching them.

Balgaire must have sensed a presence too. He stopped and turned sharply. As he raised his wand, the watcher scuttled away and was lost in the maze of darkness. Whoever, or whatever it was, was scrawny, not very tall, about four feet. And ugly. The incident was over in seconds and Larna was thankful Aron hadn't noticed anything amiss. They continued, picking up speed again, still in the light and still in a northerly direction. It wasn't long before they came to a clearing and saw a strange-looking house straight ahead. It was most peculiar with a shiny blue roof and an upside-down appearance. There were windows of all different shapes and sizes, more downstairs than up. The frames were blue, just like Balgaire's hair. The chimney pot was on the side of the house, not on the roof. The front door was also blue, and circular. Matching shiny blue roof tiles were also attached to the lower section of the structure, completing the illusion of a topsy-turvy house. The garden had an abundance of the most beautiful and unusual flowers they'd ever seen. There were some large yellow flowers that appeared to grow in the shape of a smile. Truly amazing. The wizard noticed Larna's reaction and smiled.

"Do you like my yellow beauties?" he asked. "I needed to surround myself with bright, cheerful things to remind me that there is still goodness and hope in the world. What better than to wake up and start each day with a huge smile from the flowers in my garden. I call them my Happy Blooms. Good idea, yes?"

"Did you conjure these up?" asked Larna in amazement.

"Why, yes of course, but I prefer to call it magic." He made it sound as though it were the most natural thing in the world, to give nature a helping hand and wish things into existence. "I just waved and there they were. I'd love to show you how I do it, but we don't have the leisure. Quickly, come inside."

Approaching the front of the house, Balgaire pointed and the tiny round door opened immediately. Larna thought he was going to have a problem bending and squeezing through it, but the door reshaped itself to his exact height and width as he walked through it. The same thing happened with Aron and herself. The others followed, obviously used to this phenomenon.

"Wow!" Aron's eyes widened. "I wish our doors at home would do that. My friends would be green with envy."

Once everyone was inside, Balgaire cocked his head on one side and cupped his ear with his right hand, listening intently for something. Then he relaxed.

"We are safe here for the moment," he said.

CHAPTER ELEVEN

"**W**elcome to my humble abode," said Balgaire. It was obvious that he was very proud of his home. Sniffing the air Larna detected a faint whiff of lavender which reminded her of her mother. Suddenly she felt homesick. She felt an overwhelming urge to see her.

"Ah... you're missing your mother, Larna."

"How did he know?" Larna said to Aron. "Can he read minds as well?"

Balgaire tapped the side of his nose and grinned. "Have you forgotten who I am already? I'm a wizard, with many skills. Reading thoughts and sensing moods are just two of my talents." He waved them to various chairs, flipping his hands down for them to sit. "Although sometimes I have great difficulty, depending on the person. Happily, you and your brother are very easy to read, whatever you'r feeling."

Raising her face and closing her eyes Larna breathed in the lavender perfume. "You... ?"

"That's right, I sensed you needed a gentle reminder of home," he answered softly. Before Aron could stop himself, he blurted out "I know Larna has asked you this before but, are you absolutely sure you don't have the power to rid this world of Mordrog... and the mutation epidemic, or whatever it is?"

"I'm flattered you think I'm all powerful, Aron. That is far from the truth, unfortunately. My powers are somewhat limited where Mordrog is concerned. I can't always," with a flourish of his hands, "magic away disasters that are man-made. I *have* tried, mind you, and it's very frustrating, believe me." He flopped unceremoniously into a huge, comfortable, winged chair.

There was another silence, broken by Annie slapping the

palms of her hands on her knees and standing up. "After the strain of Mordrog's unwelcome appearance," she said brightly, "I think it's time for a little more refreshment, don't you?" Everyone nodded. Anything to break the tension everyone was feeling. Larna could sense Annie was trying to be cheerful for their benefit but she could see that Chet and Tiblou were very worried. Only Balgaire seemed to be cool and calm. An assortment of mugs appeared on an ornamental coffee table in front of the boys. Larna picked up a sparkling blue mug nearest to her and handed it to Aron for the first sip.

"Mmm, hot chocolate." He wafted his mouth with his other hand to cool it, then passed the mug to his sister. Larna blew on the hot liquid, sniffed and took a deep breath before gingerly taking her first mouthful.

"Great! Vanilla milkshake... er... it's not hot. It's ice cold!" She still couldn't get used to this weirdness. "These mugs are fantastic. I'd love to take one home." She drank half of the milkshake and handed the mug back to Aron, who was beginning to get impatient for some more hot chocolate.

Suddenly, Balgaire jumped up from his chair. "We must change rooms *IMMEDIATELY!*" he shouted. Larna and Aron wanted to ask why but others stood and quickly formed a circle round them. "All will become clear," the wizard promised, clapped his hands twice and mumbling something Larna couldn't understand. Next moment they were transported into another room which went from pitch black to soft light as soon as they entered.

It was several seconds before Larna and Aron recovered from the shock of being physically teleported from one place to another. Their first time. Aron let out a huge breath. The transition wasn't at all unpleasant, but it was a shock and Larna felt weird landing in a different place. The first thing she realised was that they were in a circular room without windows or doors. The walls were light blue, reminiscent of a summer sky. Most of the furniture looked very old and comprised of two huge armchairs, like Tiblou's, and a cherry-red chaise longue. A round table was in the middle. The polished surface was painted with exotic birds.

What fascinated Larna the most was a fish tank circling the room. She'd never seen tropical fish like them. One in particular took her interest. It was deep purple with yellow tiger stripes from head to tail, all three tails in fact. Others swam up with identical striping but in different colours, green, gold and pink. Balgaire noticed her interest and asked if she'd like to put her hand in the tank, assuring her that the fish wouldn't bite.

"You'll have a pleasant surprise."

Larna was more than a bit apprehensive, after all the strange things she'd seen already, but stepped forward regardless. No matter how closely she looked for an opening, there wasn't one. Baffled, she couldn't detect any glass either, nor anything else holding back the water. She turned to Tiblou who was grinning at her reaction. Larna was one of those people whose facial expressions spoke volumes.

"Go on, put your hand in." Tiblou nodded towards the glassless tank.

Twice Larna extended her arm, drawing it swiftly back. Tibs took her by the elbow and propelled her arm forward until it went through the side, without puncturing it, and into the water. Her fingers felt as though they were moving against soft silk, not trawling through liquid. This was awesome! The striped fish swam to her and playfully nibbled her fingers which caused her to let out a muted laugh. The fish tickled as they bobbed back and forth, gently butting with their noses. Slowly pulling out, Larna's hand felt dry and she marvelled at Balgaire's extraordinary imagination that could create such an amazing aquarium.

Balgaire had been smiling at Larna's reactions, but his merriment suddenly vanished and he became serious.

"We are wasting time, my friends," he said. "Let us not forget the purpose of our visit here."

Aron felt himself begin to shake. Even though he'd readily agreed he was terrified at the thought of giving blood. He looked across at his sister and noticed she was also squirming in her seat. Balagaire read their thoughts immediately.

"There's nothing whatsoever to be afraid of," he said, soothingly.

"Whatever the procedure is in your time, here it takes only a second," added Annie. "Literally a blink of an eye."
Larna had an irrational, vision of tubes and plugs and electricity shooting from one to another, being strapped down and experimented on like Frankenstein's monster. Balgaire laughed at her fear.

"Nothing so barbaric, Larna. That was fiction ; this is reality... and it's painless. You won't even realise its being done, I promise."

These reassurances and the knowledge that what they were doing could transform the lives of hundreds of people made Larna and Aron agree to proceed. Balgaire told them to sit back in their chairs and relax. Larna was to stretch out her right arm and Aron to stretch out his left onto the edge of the chairs' arms. They did, shutting their eyes, but not before Larna saw the wizard open a heavy old book and remove two crystal vials from the silk lined hollowed-out middle. Sensing a sudden change in the atmosphere, her eyes snapped open and she saw Violet appear. Balgaire looked startled. She flew to his ear and whispered. He looked very worried and returned the two crystal containers back inside the book, clearly changing his mind.

"Mordrog is coming. Violet senses a presence and it's getting stronger by the minute. We'll have to leave this for now. I must psych myself up – your vernacular – in an effort to keep control of the situation." He placed himself in front of them. Tiblou was a pace behind and both looked up at the ceiling. Balgaire closed his eyes and stood frozen, like a statue, completely still and silent. Tilting her head backwards Larna noticed that the ceiling had miraculously darkened to resemble a clear night sky with hundreds of stars which appeared to be twinkling. It was awesome against the sky blue walls. Annie and Chet remained in the background, very quiet, as unobtrusive as possible.

Then everything around them began to shake and there was a tremendous bang. A big cloud of black smoke stung their eyes, making them water and causing a fit of coughing. Out of the confusion and ensuing vapour, Mordrog appeared. The room turned ice cold and, in that second, Larna and Aron knew that evil had entered the room.

"How did you break through the seal?" Balgaire asked, shaking with rage.

"I didn't," the warlock sneered. "I'm not with you physically." He turned to Aron, holding out his hand and gazing into his eyes. "Touch me, boy!" he commanded.

"No, DON'T!" yelled Balgaire, horrified to see a mesmerised Aron begin to raise his arm and lean forward towards the apparition. "If you do, he'll be able to enter your body." Balgaire moved between them, breaking the spell. Aron's arm dropped like a brick and he immediately sat on his hands. Larna could see the alarm on her brother's face. Hers looked equally terrified.

* * *

Tiblou gently touched Larna and Aron on the shoulders and beckoned them to follow him, an unnecessary finger to his lips. Balgaire was giving them the chance to escape by drawing Mordrog's attention away from them. They didn't need telling twice.

Slowly and silently the three of them backed towards the glassless fish tank. Tibs grabbed their hands and yanked them backwards into the silky substance. This time the fish kept their distance. Instinct took over and not wanting to drown, Aron and Larna automatically held their breath until Tiblou mimed for them to keep breathing. They let the air out of their lungs and tentatively drew in a shallow breath. Then another, until their lungs were full. Relief flooded through them with the realisation they could breathe. The trio ploughed on through the fish. A staircase suddenly materialised and Tibs pushed them towards it. As they began to climb, Larna heard snatches of heated arguments behind them. Mordrog's voice sounded threatening and Larna turned for a final look. The warlock's arms were outstretched, fingertips starting to glow and his cold eyes screwed into slits, as he stared menacingly at Balgaire.

The wizard stood erect and unwavering. He raised his wand. "Know this, Mordrog, you will *never* have power over those two youngsters. Leave this place, leave us in peace. You forfeited all privileges the day you turned towards the Dark Side and committed the worst betrayal of all by enslaving our people for gain. My home is sacrosanct, so leave it now and re-join your physical being." Balgaire waved his wand, but Mordog's image moved faster and counteracted the spell. At this, Tibs motioned to Larna and Aron to run. The warlock's triumphant laughter followed them up the stairs. As quickly as the door below closed, another miraculously opened above.

Larna didn't have time to worry about what they'd left behind because Tiblou grabbed their hands again and dragged them up the remaining steps. The backs of their legs began to ache as they raced up what seemed like hundreds of steps. The stairs led them straight back to the original room with the tiny door. Bent double, hands on knees, they tried to get their breath back, but Tibs pushed them on across the room towards the portal. Once again the doorway shaped itself to their height and size as they ran hell-for-leather through it into the open air.

When they were a safe distance from Balgaire's home, Tiblou slowed down and stopped. He was also out of breath.

"We'll... have to... return you... to your own time... until it's safe to come back... Then Balgaire will be able to complete the reversal programme."

So they moved on with an even greater sense of urgency. Clouds had formed, making the sky appear darker. Larna felt chilled to the bone. She shivered and hoped it wasn't a bad omen. There seemed to be shadows within shadows amongst the trees and she felt eyes boring into the back of her head. She wasn't about to stop and look, except for a quick glance over her shoulder whilst on the run. But, being the clumsy one in the family, she fell over some tree roots that resembled tentacles in the partial darkness. Tiblou picked her up and they continued running.

Distracted by something moving about in her pocket, Larna almost fell again. Digging deep, she pulled out the glittering red key which stopped her in her tracks. How on earth had it got there without her knowledge? There was no time to worry about it now. It was vibrating like crazy and Larna had no idea if it was trying to communicate or how to stop it. The others came to a halt as well and looked at the key.

"It's telling you that we're very close to where you jumped through," explained Tibs. Sure enough, Larna recognised their surroundings and some of the unusual trees. Within a few seconds, heat from the glowing key spread throughout her body and the chill of a few minutes earlier soon left. Her hand felt so hot that she had an overwhelming urge to blow on it or shake it until it was cool, but the key agitated so much it almost jumped from her hand. She grasped it even tighter.

Standing once again in the middle of the clearing, they turned and faced Tiblou, ready for their departure. Although they'd only known him for a few hours, it seemed much longer. Tibs was special and they were both sad to be saying goodbye. Then Clementine appeared from behind the trunk of the nearest tree and came over to them.

"Well, hello. I wasn't expecting you back so soon. But judging from the state of you, I deduce there is a problem."

"In a word, Mordrog."

"Aah! Why am I not surprised? I sensed a presence a little while ago. I take it Larna and Aron are going back to their own time?"

"As quickly as possible. Balgaire is keeping Mordrog occupied to give these two time to escape, but for how long... " His voice cracked; he couldn't finish. Sensing the urgency, Clementine became business-like. "Right, come on then. You can explain what's happened when they've safely gone." To Larna and Aron, "Can you remember what to do?"

Aron nodded vigorously. Tiblou glanced about, motioning them to get a move on, and from the look on his face Larna could tell that something else was up. She held onto the key as if their lives depended on it, which it did. The sky darkened to purple as they called out their goodbyes. Larna wondered how long it would be before they were summoned back.

"See you again as soon as it's safe," Tiblou said, then shooed them on their way with his hands. "Go, go, go!"

Larna nodded and sought Aron's hand. In a rush, he began, *"ELLA VITA, ELLA VITA, ELLA VITA... "* The ground rumbled and began to shake as the monolith rose in front of them.

Raising her left arm, Larna inserted the key, turned it and the door began to open. With a nod to Aron and a final wave to Tibs, she shut her eyes as they took their first step. But, at that moment, an incredibly strong wind whipped the leaves upwards into Larna's face, choking her. Unable to breathe properly, she attempted to spit them out of her mouth, but it didn't work and so unwittingly she used her right hand to clear them out. A feeling of being sucked backwards halted her for just a fraction of a second, then she was catapulted the rest of the way through.

As suddenly as the tornado started, it stopped leaving a deadly quiet in its wake. Larna opened her eyes. Home! She gave a sigh of relief, only to be greeted by a familiar voice nervously asking, "Where's Aron?" Looking round, Larna caught Clem's final stage of change from bird to odd-bod man.

"What do you mean? Aron's right here... " she said, expecting her brother to be by her side. But he wasn't there and Larna remembered with horror she had let go of his hand a few seconds before they leapt back through time.

"Oh no, oh no, oh no... " she gasped as the blood drained from her face and she began to shake. "What have I done?" Half of her hoped Aron was just mucking around as usual and would jump out from behind a tree. The other half knew that he wouldn't.

At that precise moment, Larna spotted Neve hurrying towards them and her heart began to thump wildly. What was she going to tell her? How could she explain why Aron wasn't with her? She could have cried. Then another thought sprang into her head. How did Yaya know where to find them?

In spite of being out of breath, Neve managed to ask, "Where have you been? You promised you wouldn't venture past the big tree." She stopped and acknowledged Clem. Tears sprang into Larna's eyes and she began to stutter. "Yaya... I... "

"This is not like you, Larna. I'm very disappointed. You've let me down." And then she softened. "Are you alright, dear? You look very pale. Where's Aron?"

After all they'd been through and leaving her kid brother behind, she couldn't hold the tears back any longer and flung her arms round her grandmother.

"I've lost him, Yaya. I don't know where he is and I'm really, really scared."

"What are you talking about?"

"You wouldn't believe in a millions years where we've been. He isn't here and I don't think he'll be coming back."

The look of horror on Clem's face said it all.

CHAPTER TWELVE

"You must go back as soon as possible," whispered Clem. "It's the only way to find Aron and bring him home."

"What about Neve?" Larna sniffed and wiped her eyes on the back of her hands.

"She thinks he's lost in the forest. Play along with that."

"Thanks Clem." She whispered.

"I'll go and contact Lee, the Forest Ranger to help search for Aron." Neve said sharply.

Larna turned to her grandmother. "I'll stay and look for my brother."

Neve hurried away, quick-marching out of the circle and disappeared into the trees.

Larna turned back to Clem. "IS there a chance of getting Aron back, then?" she asked.

"I'm not sure, but Balgaire has just communicated that in order to find Aron with the utmost haste you have to return immediately."

"Where is Aron?" Fear crept back into Larna's voice.

"Balgaire said you are not to panic, but to tell you time is of the essence. His delaying spell wasn't successful and Mordrog escaped. The warlock found you as you were about to leave and pulled Aron from your grasp at the last minute."

"I've *got* to return, then."

"Yes, I'm afraid so. You've still got the key?"

"I've been hanging on to it for dear life. But I didn't think I was allowed to leap on my own."

Clem rubbed his chin and thought for a few seconds. "Strictly speaking, I'm not supposed to do it, but on this occasion I'll leap with you. Otherwise you may not make it. I'll say the words. Ready?"

"Yeah, but hurry."

They stepped back into the circle and Clem began to chant, *"ELLA VITA, ELLA VITA, ELLA VITA... "*

The now-familiar rumble underground signalled the appearance of the door. Larna hastily placed the key in the lock and turned. As before, it opened and she was about to dash through, but Clem held her back.

"Careful, girl, you don't know what's waiting for you." He grasped her elbow and escorted her through the portal.

Tiblou was on the other side, waiting for them. His worried expression showed the seriousness of the situation. "I feel I'm to blame for this, Larna. If we hadn't found a way to bring you here, you'd still be oblivious to our problems, back in your own time, safe and happy with your brother and family."

"If it's any consolation, Tibs, I don't blame anybody but myself. But now I just want to find my brother and take him home."

"Yes, indeed! We must head back to Balgaire's immediately. He's waiting for us. Hopefully he's managed to come up with a plan of action."

Leaving Clem to return to the other side of the portal, they headed off. Larna's feet were on autopilot whilst her head was full of 'what ifs', coming up with the worst possible scenarios. She felt gutted. Empty. They picked up speed until they were practically running. Balgaire's home was dead ahead, though Larna didn't recognise the surroundings. The Happy Blooms were shut tight and their heads drooped. Not smiling any more. It suddenly dawned on Larna that he'd also moved the house. Literally. The tiny door opened and moulded itself to their shapes before letting them in. Balgaire, Annie and Chet had returned to the first room which was expanding and contracting as the wizard paced up and down. Violet appeared and sat cross legged on the top of a chair-back.

Larna stood quietly and watched. Balgaire turned and ran both sets of fingers through his already untidy hair. He looked directly at Tiblou and asked, "Were you followed?"

"I'm not sure. Why?"

"Violet senses an evil presence again, and we fear it could be Edsel this time."

"Who's Edsel?" Larna enquired.

"He's Mordrog's assistant, his second-in-command. The closest description I can give you is a troll. He's monstrously cruel and has no conscience which makes him a perfect foil for the warlock. He's a nasty piece of work."

"Is he the one spying on us?"

The wizard sighed. "I believe so. It's the only logical explanation for certain things that have been happening to you… "

"What, like causing me to trip up more than usual?"

"Probably. Yes. I think you're beginning to realise what an evil little devil he can be. He can send you down the wrong path until you're lost. Make you fall. His tricks aren't very original but it amuses his tiny mind to cause chaos and confusion. But don't be fooled by his juvenile tricks. He is dangerous and never to be underestimated. Nothing happens that isn't reported back to Mordrog. He is his master's eyes and ears."

"I see. Well, I don't think we were being watched on the way here. I didn't sense anything, not like before."

"That's good."

"What's happened to Aron?" demanded Larna. "Where is he?"

Balgaire took hold of her hand and led her forwards. "Come with me."

Larna followed him into the next room, amazed to find it was completely empty except for two chairs in the middle placed back to back, each one facing a huge mirrored wall. It was several seconds before Larna realised neither of the mirrors showed a reflection. Just an empty void. It was very strange. Balgaire went and sat on one of the chairs. "This mirror depicts what *has* been and the other what *will* be." His voice was sombre.

"Are you telling me I can see into the past?"

"That is what I have just said." He raised his hand. "But no, Larna, you can't change what has already happened."

Larna started to turn the chair round so that she could sit next to Balgaire.

"DON'T TOUCH THE CHAIR!" yelled the wizard. "That one *must* remain facing the other way, to the future."

"Why?"

"Because if the chairs are placed side by side, depending which way they face, there will be no future... or past."

"And if they face each other... ?"

"There will be nothing... just oblivion. No past. No future. No anything."

Larna snatched her hand away; an electric current had run up her arm as she touched the chair. It sent her reeling backwards with some force. Unable to stop, she fell against the mirror. On and on and on and through it. She could see Balgaire on the other side, watching and nodding. Her arms wind-milling like crazy as she tried to regain her balance.

She found herself in the clearing again and saw that she and Aron were getting ready to leap, their eyes tightly shut. She was watching everything happen for a second time, like an action replay. It was a peculiar feeling, yet she was fascinated. An agitated Tiblou and Clementine were watching helplessly as the leaves swirled round them, gathering momentum, and Larna tried to spit them out of her mouth. Then she saw them swirling round her brother, encasing him until only his outstretched hand was visible. Larna heard herself coughing and spitting. Then up came her hand to clear her mouth and nostrils of the dead leaves so she could breathe. This time, though, she *knew* she'd let go of Aron's hand. She heard his cry, *"Laaarna... "* Then Mordrog's maniacal laugh as Aron's body floated away. And, in that second, Larna leapt.

CHAPTER THIRTEEN

Nobody said a word as Larna relived what she'd just seen. Her legs felt like rubber and began to buckle, so she sat on the floor at Balgaire's feet, looking helplessly up at him.

"Now you know the truth, Larna." The wizard spoke softly and looked genuinely concerned. "But don't blame yourself too much. Mordrog's the real reason why this happened."

With tears streaming down her cheeks Larna asked, "Is Aron dead?"

"No. Your brother is somewhere very close to Mordrog and I believe he is in a cryogenic state... "

"What does that mean?" she interrupted.

"It means he's deeply unconscious, as if frozen," explained Balgaire. "But he's unharmed... for now. What we don't know is Mordrog's plan for Aron. My immediate guess is that he will try moral blackmail, using your brother to entice you to him. We must avoid that at all costs, because once he's captured you, he'll *never* let either of you go free. He can't afford to." He paused. "The good news is, whilst Aron is in that state, he won't be aware of anything, nor can anything hurt him." Balgaire bent and put both hands on Larna's shoulders. "Trust me. We *will* find a way to bring Aron safely back, but I need the others to help me." He stood, drawing Larna up at the same time. "Come," was all he said and, still numb with shock, she followed meekly as a lamb.

They went back into the first room. Annie, Tiblou and Chet were seated as they'd left them and all three looked as worried as she felt. Their sympathy almost made Larna break down again. Balgaire clapped his hands twice, startling her out of her self-pity. "It's time, so pay attention, Larna. I need the four of you to hold hands, circling me, and to channel your thoughts on to our unfortunate young friend while I concentrate all my kinetic energy locating Mordrog." He looked intently at each one of them. "When – or rather, if – I am successful, I'll transport myself to that location and try to break whatever spell the warlock has placed over Aron."

They positioned themselves round the wizard and clasped their hands, looking to him for further instructions. "Retribution is long overdue for all the death and destruction this warlock has caused," Balgaire said grimly. "Mordrog's reign of terror *must* be brought to an end. And, to relieve him of his obscene wealth will be an added bonus." He looked knowingly at Tibs, "Should I fail, you have your instructions."

Larna shot an involuntary look at Balgaire. "What do you mean, should you fail?"

"You must have realised by now that there can only be one outcome to this conflict. If I am victorious, there will be a happy outcome, but if that greedy criminal wins the battle... I will lose... everything... "

Larna was appalled and dropped her hands, breaking the circle. "What will happen then?" she asked in a horrified whisper.

"Tiblou has been my pupil since he was very young and knows what to do, should I not return." Balgaire's voice hardened, "And, as time is of the essence, my girl, I suggest you focus on your brother with the others to break Mordrog's concentration. I *must* get into his head and see where they are. Once that happens the element of surprise will be gone and he will take evasive action. So you must all be vigilant and expect the unexpected. And *do not* break the circle until I know where Aron is being held. Only then can you join me. I cannot stress enough, Tiblou, that you must take charge... should I fail."

Larna's mind was in turmoil. How could Tibs take over when he wasn't a wizard? She had forgotten Balgaire could read her mind. "These matters are not your concern, Larna," he said. "Now please concentrate." Angry that her thoughts were no longer her own, Larna tried to hide the swearing in her mind, but knew it wouldn't have gone unnoticed too. Nevertheless, she held out her hands to the others again. Balgaire raised his eyes skywards and gently rocked back and forth. The wizard lowered his arms to his sides. Larna noticed a wand appear in his right hand. She looked at it curiously, wondering what it would feel like to hold it in her hand and maybe use it to cast a spell...

"Larna! Stop daydreaming." The sharp words in her mind brought her back to the task in hand and she realised one of them had mentally told her off. The others had their heads bowed, eyes shut, and she was about to follow suit when out of the corner of her eye she noticed something move. Quite naturally, she whipped her head round and was just in time to see an ugly face peering in through the window. Larna jumped, breaking the circle. She was sure it was Edsel. His eyes were still bright greeny/yellow and the look on his face was pure evil. He had a long pointed hook-shaped nose, his skin was dull and lifeless with a tinge of green in it. She could only see his clothing from the waist up. It looked dirty and ill-fitting. Larna had the impression that underneath the robes he was very scrawny.

The others opened their eyes and turned towards the window, but the creature had scurried away the instant his eyes met Larna's. Balgaire ran to close some wooden shutters that suddenly appeared out of thin air. The same happened to the other three windows, plunging the room into complete darkness. A rush of air beside Larna's ear turned out to be Balgaire waving his wand, flooding the room with warm amber light.

"That was Edsel, wasn't it? The creature in the woods, watching us all the time."

"Correct."

"He gives me the creeps."

"Come now. We have to hurry. At this very minute Edsel is rushing to tell his master what he has learned. I only hope we aren't too late." Balgaire ushered them back into a circle. "This will have to be a one and only attempt. Agreed?" Then, without waiting for a reply, "Are you ready?"

They nodded. Then Violet materialised and flew round the room sprinkling some glowing dust on them, then settled on the back of a chair, legs dangling. She gave Larna a beautiful smile which lit up her face and the teenager couldn't help smiling back before closing her eyes. Instantly, a picture of Aron floated into her mind and she felt a jolt in her chest. She missed him so much. Another image crept in, of her brother aged five, on a bike ride. She remembered the injuries he'd sustained when he forgot to use his brakes downhill and ploughed head-first into a farmer's gate. His five-year-old classmates thought he'd been in a punch-up and wanted to be best friends. "I got respect!" had been his proud boast. Then she experienced a sudden rush of fear as someone else's jumbled thoughts crowded into her head and ousted her own. With a shake of her head they eventually cleared, leaving an image of Aron fast asleep. Realisation dawned. Her friends had helped channel Larna's thoughts in the right direction, until they'd found him.

"I know where they are!" Tiblou sounded excited.

Being last to open her eyes, Larna was last to realise Balgaire and Violet had already vanished. Tiblou beckoned the others to follow him to the front door, but as they reached it they noticed the large key slowly turning in the lock, then heard bolts shooting into place. Grossly annoyed with himself, Tibs kicked the door, "I should've seen that coming. Edsel has locked us in! " He tried turning the key but couldn't budge it. Crossing to the door, Larna had a go, with all her strength. Nothing happened, so she put her foot against the wall and pulled on the door handle. That didn't work either. Chet charged at it with his shoulder, bounced back and fell onto the floor. Larna, indignant, decided to have another go. All of a sudden, the door blew inwards with some force sending her flying backwards against the opposite wall. Tibs pulled Annie and Chet out of the way just in time to prevent them being flattened.

As fast as the door blew in, it shut tight again. Larna staggered to her feet and even though she knew it wouldn't do any good, she yelled and charged at the door, more out of frustration than bravado. The same thing happened again, only this time the door almost knocked her out and she only just managed to avoid injury by leaping backwards out of the way. Clearly, this was a battle Larna wasn't going to win, so she tried opening one of the shutters instead. Chet had the same idea, but they were all stuck fast. The room was a prison.

"Tiblou... get me out of here! I've *got* to find my brother and take him home." Larna was almost in hysterics, her anger and frustration turning to panic as the light in the room also started to dim. "Tiblou! *Do* something!"

"Calm down, Larna, you aren't helping the situation any." The sharpness of Tibs's voice pulled her up sharply, making her see reason. "I need absolute silence so that I can focus." He pressed his fingers to his temples and closed his eyes as the light went out leaving them in complete darkness.

Within a few seconds, there was a gentle pat on Larna's back as Tiblou said, "There *is* a way out. I've just seen it. Everybody hold hands. Larna, you hold on to me. Okay? Now walk, quick as you can, without falling. Ready, then?" She nodded vigorously and obeyed. A glowing speck of light appeared which began to pulsate rapidly, getting larger and larger, closer and closer, until it shimmered into focus. It was a bright red door. Tiblou easily turned the handle and the door swung open. Larna squinted, trying to see what was on the other side. It was a cupboard. A very small one. Bewildered, she whispered, "This is just another... dead-end." Her heart did a somersault and landed in the pit of her stomach. Optimism turned to despair in the blink of an eye.

CHAPTER FOURTEEN

"There's no way out of here!" Larna leaned against the wall and looked challengingly at Tibs. "You *said* this was the way out!"

"Ssssh, Larna! Don't be such a defeatist, have a bit more faith." He walked into the cupboard, turned and beckoned the rest of them in. "Hurry up, we haven't much time."

"I really don't think... "

Tibs and Chet grabbed Larna's arms and yanked her inside, whilst Annie pushed her unceremoniously from behind. They had to inhale and hold as the door closed, locking them in. The cupboard began to shake, then it dropped like a stone. This felt terrifying and Annie squeezed Larna's hand reassuringly. As the contraption thudded to a full stop, like a lift, her knees would have buckled if the four of them hadn't been so tightly jammed in.

"That wasn't so bad now, was it?" Annie said, more to herself than anyone else, regaining her composure by patting down her hair.

The door swung open and they fell out into what looked like a corridor. The glow from inside the cupboard only lit a short distance before fading into darkness. On wobbly legs, Annie took the first steps along the narrow passage, leaning heavily on Chet's arm for support. Larna and Tibs followed. Every so often the lights came on in front and went out behind, but Larna still couldn't see the end of the tunnel. Sticking closely to Tiblou, she wasn't going to let him out of her sight.

"What happens next? Where do we go from here?" she asked.

"Hopefully, outside." Chet sounded unsure, speaking to Larna over his shoulder.

"Eventually," Larna added sarcastically, concentrating on not getting left behind. The corridor seemed never-ending.

A glint to the left caught Larna's eye. When the next light flashed on, she saw huge portraits in chunky gold frames on both sides of the corridor, stretching as far as she could see. Each person was painted wearing a beautiful robe in dazzling colours. Larna slowed down to admire them. What struck her most was that they all held their heads high, proud and aristocratic. She thought the women may have been witches, each one with lovely flowing hair to their waist; blondes, brunettes, or fiery coppers. She also noticed that in every picture there was a small figure, not unlike Violet, in various poses alongside the main characters, just as colourful and proud.

The last portrait on the left showed a much younger Balgaire. He had a gentle smile on his face and looked the part, head high and shoulders back. Opposite was a large gold frame, with a blank canvas mounted inside. Larna assumed it was waiting for the next witch or wizard to be painted once Balgaire's time was up. She shivered, not wanting to think of that. As she gazed into the empty mount, her own reflection looked back! She jumped, bumping into Tiblou who was just in front of her. She pointed at the picture, but when she looked at it again there was nothing, just a blank canvas under glass.

"Sorry, Tibs," she said. "I'm seeing things now!"

At the end of the corridor, a flight of stairs became visible, going up to a tiny speck of light which seemed to be getting brighter and redder. Tiblou lead the way, urging everyone to move faster. A glowing red door appeared to be gliding down the stairs towards them as they climbed up to meet it. It silently opened outward and a blast of cool air rushed in. Tibs ushered them through the door which closed behind them then faded to a pinprick before vanishing into thin air like a puff of smoke.

Time had passed so quickly that day had turned to night. They hurried into the woods, hoping Edsel hadn't seen them escape. The sky was filled with millions of stars, some bright enough to light their path through the trees. They tried hard not to make a noise, but it was an almost impossible task. Settling down, they walked at a fast pace, kicking up leaves each time they accidentally strayed from the path. The now-familiar scent from the foliage became stronger, reminding Larna of Mordrog and, by association, Aron. The thought of him made her quicken her pace, knowing they were getting closer to where her brother was being held captive. But the others couldn't keep up. The party slowed to a snail's pace because Annie was in some difficulty.

"I'm so sorry to hold everybody up." She said, looking exhausted and pale. "Give me a few minutes to catch my breath. If you like, you three can go on ahead and I'll catch you up."

"No way!" exclaimed Larna.

"Of course not," Tiblou agreed. "Besides, we're very close now and must stick together at all costs. So no more nonsense mother, okay? It isn't safe here for any of us."

They moved on again. Suddenly, Larna tripped and fell hard, grazing her knees. As soon as she saw her own blood, her pulse began to race and she felt faint.

"Are you alright?" asked Chet, helping her gently to her feet. "I think Edsel may have found us. He can move remarkably fast for a deformed creature. We warned you, he enjoys playing cruel games and tricking people. He's probably laughing at us right now."

"Pack it in, Edsel!" Larna shouted out angrily. "I know all about you now." She didn't know if the creature had heard, but she didn't fall down again.

Having tied a hanky round the gash in one of her knees, they carried on walking until they were met by what appeared to be a mini-tornado. Annie's hair blew loose, whipping her face, and everyone's clothes became plastered to their bodies. The group held hands again so they wouldn't be separated or pulled into it. Then they saw where the wind was coming from. Larna's jaw dropped at the scene in front of her.

* * *

Balgaire and Mordrog were standing two or three feet apart glaring at each other. Larna and the others approached as quietly as possible, creeping forwards until they were standing directly behind Balgaire. They let go of each other's hands. Tibs nudged

Larna's arm and nodded towards a roofless wishing-well that stood in the centre of the clearing. When Larna's eyes followed his pointing finger upwards, she thought her heart would stop beating. There was Aron! They had found him! The boy was floating on his back, arms to his sides on a cushion of air above the well, seemingly in a deep and peaceful sleep.

Before she could stop herself, Larna yelled "ARON!" at the top of her voice and charged towards Mordrog, screaming like a banshee. The warlock calmly waved his wand anti-clockwise and pointed it straight at the girl. A rush of freezing cold air hit Larna full force in the stomach, blasting her right off her feet. She sailed backwards through the air and hit the ground, doubled-up with pain. It was a full minute before her breath, and her sanity returned to normal. She realised she'd had a very lucky escape landing between two trees and guessed that Balgaire had intervened to assist her landing. She stood up, legs like jelly and teeth chattering like castanets. Seeing Mordrog laughing at her, Larna's anger boiled up again but Annie grabbed her arm to prevent her trying any more stupid tricks.

"Leave it to Balgaire, dear. He's the only one who can save your brother, I'm afraid."

Larna knew she was right. If she caused any further trouble, Mordrog would only make things even more difficult for Aron.

At least Larna's intervention had given Balgaire time to compose himself. He stepped forwards, ready to go on the attack, but his opponent reacted immediately and set about defending himself. Wizard and warlock simultaneously raised their wands and chanted, *"MORTUNA MORS VOBIS!"* Mordrog also yelled, *"Die, old man! Die!"* Both flung the point of their wands in the direction of the other. A huge bang was followed by thick purple smoke which caused the others to cough and waft the air with their hands. Larna's eyes welled up, tears streamed down her cheeks and a foul-smelling luminous blue gunge oozed from her nostrils.

Eventually, her breathing became easier as the air began to clear. The tears stopped and she continuously blew her nose into an old hankie taken from her pocket. It glowed with the sticky, smelly mess. Looking around, she saw the others were also suffering the same fate. When her vision cleared sufficiently, she saw that Aron was still safely floating above the well and that Balgaire and Mordrog had cancelled each other out. They were still facing each other, shock and surprise on both their faces.

* * *

A pat on the back made Larna jump and look over her shoulder. Uncle Roger had arrived along with several customers from the café who were watching from the safety of the trees. Larna was certain Edsel was in there somewhere.

"We heard a loud bang and rushed to find out what had happened," explained Roger. "Are you OK?"

"I'm not sure how to answer that. So many things are happening just now, I really don't know." She pointed to her brother, thankfully oblivious to his plight. "I'm more concerned about Aron's safety." Her brother seemed to have been forgotten as the two magicians fought to banish each other.

"Balgaire needs to be victorious if Aron is to be freed," said Roger, wisely. "We must all will him to win."

The battle raged on with first Balgaire getting the upper hand and then Mordrog. Just when it seemed they would cancel each other out and, drained of power, they would have to fight again another day, Mordrog launched one last offensive. A sudden mighty blast of force sent Balgaire flying backwards through the air. Larna watched in horror as the wizard's body hurtled past them and hit a huge tree at such a speed that a protruding branch went straight through his back and came out of his chest. As he hung there, a trickle of blood ran down his chin and dropped onto his robe. The startled look in his eyes seemed to grow dim as he whispered his final words, "I'm so sorry... " Then the light faded from his eyes. His body went limp and heavy. The branch split and broke off. Balgaire slid down the tree and lay crumpled on the grass. He was gone. Forever.

Nobody moved. Silent shock. Until someone began to wail and gradually the air was filled with sorrowful cries. The reality of the situation hit and sank in. They had lost the only person who could have saved them. "What do we do now?" whispered Larna, burying her head in Uncle Roger's shoulder. Tiblou ran to Balgaire's side and cradled him in his arms.

"YOU ARE PURE EVIL!" Tiblou screamed. "This man took you in and looked after you like his own son. How could you do this to him? *I HATE you!"*

"Shut up, Tiblou, and get it out of my sight. Take the remains of your friend with you. *NOW!"*

The heartlessness of Mordrog's words made Larna stiffen with fury. She tried to approach the warlock, but once again found her feet wouldn't move. They felt as if they were set in a block of cement. Roger made a brave attempt to rescue Larna, but he too was stuck. Those closest tried to help as well, but found they had also suffered the same fate. They were all at his mercy.

Mordrog stood, hands on hips, studying Larna with mock concern on his face. "What *have* you started?" he chided, shaking his head. "Everything was running smoothly until you and your brother came along. Now, I realise you were given a great deal of help along the way by… " he glanced in the direction of Tiblou and the lifeless Balgaire, "but they can't help you now. The bottom line is, Larna dear, that you two represent a major threat to my plans for *their* future." He hooked his thumb in the direction of the watching crowd and shrugged. "Well, truth to tell, the *only* threat now."

Tiblou seemed to have regained some composure. From a sitting position by the tree, he called to Mordrog, "Let these two return to their world never to come back. Then they can't be a threat of any sort to you and, you will have won."

"Oh, it's far too late for that, you fool. Don't you understand? That's a chance I'm not prepared to take anymore. I have to rid myself of these unwelcome visitors forever. It's the only way I can be certain they won't come back to haunt me. I'm just looking out for my interests and those of my friends and business partners, of course." He beckoned his servant. All eyes turned to Edsel in the trees. He grinned back nervously. "Come here, my little friend. It's time."

Edsel scurried to the warlock's side as fast as his crooked little legs would let him, leaving a pungent body odour in his wake. "I'm coming as fast as I can, master," he called in his whiney voice. "What do you want of me? Is there something I can do for you?"

"Yes, my little friend." He patted Edsel's bald head. "Yes, there is. You can help rid me of these troublesome brats."
The little creature gleefully rubbed his hands together. "For... ever?"

"Naturally. We'll wipe them from the face of the earth." Mordrog warmed to his subject. "Better still, I'll erase all trace and memory of them from their world. They will never have existed. You can start by watching the lad up there and tell me when he wakes up."

As Edsel hurried over to the well, Mordrog strode over to Larna. "Look carefully upon my face, my girl, as it will be the very last one you ever see – after you've witnessed the demise of your dear brother, of course." Then, flinging up his arms, he waved the wand and began to chant, *"IN CIRCULO VORTEX"* over and over again. Larna watched in horror as Aron began to descend slowly towards the well. It was obvious he was heading for the darkness below and would never return. "Out of the arms of Morpheus, open your eyes and witness your demise," yelled the warlock, almost mad with excitement. "I need to *feel* your terror."

Edsel started jumping up and down. "He's awake, master! He's awake!" Aron opened his eyes and blinked rapidly. Only his head moved as he looked around. Not yet understanding the danger he was in, he tried to sit up and began to wobble about. In that instant his eyes registered horror as he started falling towards the well's raging vortex.

"*LARNA!*" he screamed.

"*NO!*" she roared back, struggling to move her legs. There was nothing she could do to save her brother's life. Next moment, Mordrog rounded on her, all laughter gone from his terrible face, and Larna knew that her time had come as well. She would be joining her brother inside the whirling vortex for the whole of eternity.

"*IN CURCULO...*" he began, but stopped suddenly in mid-flow and stared over his right shoulder. His jaw went slack and dropped almost onto his chest. In the middle of raising his wand arm, Mordrog suddenly froze. Literally. Somebody had intervened and cast a spell on the warlock. Larna had no idea who was still alive with that kind of power. A great rush of wind followed and her legs were freed. Everyone else discovered they could move too and began to dash towards the well. Larna stood and gawped like an idiot at the scene playing out in front of her.

CHAPTER FIFTEEN

A vision of gold with flowing blonde hair streaked past Larna heading for the well. Violet hovered above the opening, looking into its depths, and then the gold vision plunged down into the swirling vortex. She returned carrying Aron. He looked lifeless cradled in her arms. Then she gently laid him on the grass, stroked his forehead and bent down to blow life-giving air into his lungs.

Larna ran to his side and knelt on the grass. Taking her brother's cold limp hand in hers, she tried rubbing some warmth back into it, whispering, "Don't die on me, Aron. Please don't die... " Tears streamed down her cheeks and dropped off her chin onto their clasped hands just as Violet's hair fell forward and covered them. A twitch was the first sign that Aron was going to be all right. Then a massive intake of breath followed by coughs and splutters as he spat out a stream of purple fluid. Larna laughed hysterically. "He's back!" she shouted to everybody and nobody. "Aron's *ALIVE!*"

Excitement rippled through the crowd around them and Larna raised her dirty face to thank the miracle worker. Violet pushed her hair back and gave her the biggest grin Larna had ever seen. An overwhelming sense of relief passed between them, but it only lasted a moment. Behind them, a cracking sound reminded them that Mordrog was still at large and managing to free himself from his frozen state.

"Well, well, well," he sneered, ambling forward shaking shards of ice from his clothes. "If my eyes don't deceive me, it's the witch from the past who thinks she's so much better than me." He stood, hands on hips, with a haughty look on his angry face. "I knew you'd come to save the day. You took your time, though. I'm surprised you didn't arrive sooner."

Larna couldn't believe her eyes. The witch standing defiantly in front of Mordrog had long blond hair, blue eyes and a very familiar face.

"Yaya, is that you?" she gasped.

"Shush, dear," soothed her grandmother. "I've come to protect you from this... monster. He can't hurt you now, I promise." Facing the warlock, she spoke in a cold, calm voice they'd never heard before. It sent chills down Larna's back. "You will never harm anyone again!"

Mordrog pulled himself up to his full height and looked down on her as if he was about to squash her under foot. "Much has changed since you were last here, Neve, and I am not alone now. See, I have my grotesque little servant." He grabbed Edsel by the shoulder and pushing him forward roughly, oblivious to the hurt on the creature's face. The warlock's voice rose as his features changed to malice. "Some people never learn. Take Balgaire. The old fool is dead because he grossly underestimated me. I've grown in strength and in power." His voice rose another notch, "NO ONE can defeat me now. And if you think you can, I challenge you to try!"

"I'm well aware of your increased powers," replied Neve coolly, "but it doesn't change anything. Someone has to stop you, so I accept your challenge. You made a grave mistake attempting to harm my grandchildren. Never underestimate the female of the species."

"Oh, no mistake. My tactics worked like a charm. What you fail to realise is that women are *so* predictable in certain circumstances – even you, Neve. I *knew* you would come to me like an avenging angel if you felt your progeny were being threatened with the ultimate."

"I see. Then I pity you." Neve shook her head sadly from side to side. "Such a talent wasted. You threw away an incredible opportunity to work alongside Balgaire and no doubt walk in his shoes one day. I know he was training you for that very purpose. But you turned to the Dark Side instead and that will be your downfall in the end."

"We'll see about that," he scoffed.

The two of them squared up to each other, the mighty warlock and the elderly white witch with a will of iron, ready to do battle. Moments later, the ground began to shake and a powerful force-field encircled the fighters, a howling wind driving everyone else away and making them to cling onto the surrounding trees to stop themselves being blown away. Standing about three feet apart, staring at each other, Mordrog and Neve both raised their wands and flung all manner of spells at each other, but Mordrog was a split-second quicker and sent the witch flying backwards in the same way he had Balgaire and Larna. It was his favourite spell and he used it all the time. But the moment the witch was blown away she returned, her hair a wild mess, a furious look on her face. Mordrog hadn't expected her to return so fast and had let his guard slip. Neve took full advantage of his lapse in concentration and her spell sent him tumbling head-over-heels until he hit the wall of the force-field. Breath whooshed out of his body like a gigantic belch and he dropped like a stone.

"Ouch... that's gotta hurt." Larna chuckled. "Go on, Yaya, give him another one."

"And one from me," added Aron.

But their smiles froze on their faces as Mordrog pulled himself together and flew back into the fight. It was obvious by the crooked way he hovered that his back had been badly hurt, but his pride was wounded even more, being knocked out by a woman – and an elderly woman at that. The look on his face was murderous. Larna could tell that Mordrog had completely lost control and would battle to the death. Neve's!

A flash of light to the right caused Larna to take her eyes off the fighters in time to see Violet battle her way through the wind and debris. She flew over to Balgaire and snuggled down into one of the huge pockets inside his blood-soaked outer garments, right over his heart. Larna wondered what she was doing, but there was no time to find out because the next round of the clash between their grandmother and Mordrog, witch against warlock, had begun. Both used their wands, each neutralising the other, forming an arc of pure electric power. Showers of sparks lit the sky which burnt holes in their clothes. The air surrounding them turned yellow. They circled each other, menacingly, faster and faster until they were just a blur. Larna's eyes ached from watching the whirling fighters and her head hurt with the exertion of it all. Then, what she'd dreaded most, happened. Neve and Mordrog came to an abrupt halt. The battle had reached its climax.

Mordrog had a twisted smile on his face whilst Neve, her long hair dishevelled, looked flustered and giddy. It dawned on Larna that Mordrog had been controlling their speed the whole time in order to disorientate her. His plan had worked because their grandmother staggered for just a fraction of a second too long and turned the wrong way, putting a hand to her head. Larna feared she was about to throw up, or worse still pass out. She and Aron were forced to watch horror-struck as Mordrog drew back his arms and violently flung a final spell at her.

"MORTUNA MORS VOBIS... DIE, DIE!" he screamed, changing his wand into a heavy globed staff and swung a crushing blow to the back of Neve's head with it. She gave a startled cry and crumpled, falling to the ground with a sickening thud. In that instant the force-field vanished and the wind blew itself out allowing the debris to settle back on the ground.

A triumphant Mordrog drifted down and stood with one foot on the witch's body, head up, arms high in the air. He began laughing like the maniac. The staff shrank to its original form. Larna waited for Neve to spring back up and yell, "Fooled You!" into the warlock's face, but she didn't. She lay perfectly still as if the life force had been sucked out of her for good. Larna ran over to help her, closely followed by Aron. Half-way there Mordrog suddenly extended his arm, fingers up, palm forward and pushed the air. The force stopped them both in their tracks and they found themselves sprawling on the ground. Clambering to their knees, in total shock, the teenager and her brother found themselves unable to speak. Balgaire was dead, Neve was dead and they were entirely at the mercy of a mad man.

CHAPTER SIXTEEN

"Yaya, wake up!" Aron yelled. "Wake UP!"

There was no response. The old lady was still breathing, but unconscious. Out cold. Mordrog had defeated her and she could play no further part in the proceedings.

Over Aron's shoulder Larna saw Violet gently rubbing Balgaire's chest. His blood dripped off her hands, pooled on the grass and began to glow as she muttered spells and incantations to herself. She felt sorry for the tiny being, trying to revive someone who was most obviously dead. But, before long, Balgaire's head twitched slightly. 'This can't be happening," Larna whispered. "It's not possible!" Then, to her utter amazement, the wizard gave an almighty shudder and took a huge breath. Larna shook Aron and turned his head to one side for him to see.

"I don't believe this!" gasped Aron. Balgaire was trying to sit up. He managed it, slowly pulling himself into an upright position. With a dazed look in his eyes, he glanced around. A few feet away, wrapped in his own success, Mordrog prodded the fallen witch once in the ribs with his foot and ,getting no response, continued laughing at the stars and marching around to the music in his head. He truly believed he had nothing more to fear. Meanwhile, Violet flew swiftly over to Neve and placed her hands on the back of her injured head. It began to glow as the fairy drew the pain out of their grandmother's skull, taking it into herself. She healed her, as she had done Balgaire.

Suddenly, Mordrog noticed what had happened to Balgaire. An incredulous look passed over his face as he watched the wizard's feeble attempts to stand up. Shaking his head in disbelief, the warlock rose up in the air to get a better view. Meanwhile,

Neve began to move, slowly at first but more easily after that. Her hair was matted with blood and her clothes reeked of burning, but she was right back to her old self. Stealthily, she floated upwards until she was parallel with him, hovering about three feet behind his back.

Larna and Aron could hardly contain their joy and had to bite their knuckles to stop themselves from shouting encouragement, giving her position away. Chet, Annie and Uncle Roger came to join them while Tiblou remained close to Balgaire until he regained his strength and could manoeuvre on his own. His clothes had turned from the bright red of fresh blood to a dull brown as it dried round the edges.

Seeing the witch's manoeuvring, Edsel tried jumping up and down to warn his master, but no amount of waving and shouting could attract the warlock's attention. Mordrog was transfixed by Balgaire's resurrection and had neither eyes nor ears for anything else. Balgaire staggered to his feet and looked up at his old adversary. It was obvious he was in great pain and held on to Tiblou whilst taking his first steps. Violet flew to his side and lightly touched his right shoulder as they began their ascent to face their common enemy. Balgaire, Violet and Neve all fixed their gaze on Mordrog. They were telepathically planning something special.

All four combatants were hampered by their injuries. Balgaire still had a stake sticking out of his chest, Neve had a matted head wound and Violet was covered with Blagaire's blood which she wore like a badge of honour. Following his heavy fall, Mordrog's spine was clearly out of kilter so he was unable to stand straight. This meant he couldn't turn round easily and remained totally unaware of the witch behind his back. None of them could cope with any further injury. So the winner this time would be the ultimate victor.

The battle began. Waving his wand in a circle as far around as his crooked back would allow and shouting a curse at Balgaire, Mordrog threw the first awful bolt. Not being fast enough to dodge it, the wizard groaned loudly as a wave of energy caught him on his left arm. The wand fell from his lifeless fingers just as

Violet raised her tiny wand and returned the force, sending Mordrog backwards so he almost bumped into Neve For several minutes the battle raged noisily. From each side, charges of deadly power created bright sparks and flames when they found their target. Those, combined with Violet's involuntary colour showers, made a vivid but terrifying sight. The smell of burning was sickening and, to everyone's dismay, the warlock seemed to have the upper hand again.

Pressing home his advantage, Mordrog released another burst of dazzling lethal energy that brought a terrible scream from Balgaire. He dropped to the ground like an old rag doll. Everyone knew for certain that this time he wouldn't get up again. Mordrog was triumphant, laughing and boasting about his conquest. But he still didn't know Neve was behind him... and Balgaire's death had been a clever ploy. Knowing Violet's healing powers could only revive him for a short while, the wizard had sacrificed his final moments to give the witch advantage of a surprise attack from the rear. Slowly and silently Neve floated nearer to the warlock, her wand morphing into a staff complete with a heavy iridescent globe on the end. Using both hands, she swung it and gave him an almighty blow to the back of his head, just as he had done to her, and with such force she nearly lost her balance. Then she delivered a crashing blow to his damaged spine. The crystal globe on the end of her staff glowed bright red with blood from Mordrog's broken skull and crippled back. He tried without success to turn and face his surprise attacker.

She pointed her staff at the staggering warlock. In a low, menacing voice she said, "*I banish you from here forever!*" The sky darkened, a brilliant ray of light filtered down and completely surrounded the snarling Mordrog. He found himself lifted up, shaken violently and turned upside down. Blood dripped and spattered everywhere from the open wound to the back of his head as he was carried over towards the well. Realising his fate, a blood-curdling scream escaped his lips as he hovered above the gaping black hole. Flames shot up from the vortex, binding him in a vice-like grip, slowly drawing him down towards oblivion.

As Mordrog's body neared the well-head, Edsel dashed to the edge and leaned over. "Master, master," he yelled, leaning as far as he dare without falling in. "Come back to me! Come back to me!" He grabbed Mordrog's cloak and pulled him back through the flames. But this was no act of compassion, no desperate action of a servant about to lose his beloved master. It was an act of heartless self-interest. After an unseemly tug of war, Edsel seized the warlock's prized possession, his smooth black wand, and gave him a mighty push to send him on his way. Jumping down, Edsel punched the air shouting, "YES-S-S!" and ran past everyone, disappearing into the forest as fast as his crooked legs would carry him, his large knobbly head bobbing excitedly from side to side.

Then everyone was drawn back to Mordrog's demise by a plaintive cry echoing from below as he plunged downwards at speed. That was the last they ever heard from the warlock because the well started to vanish, as if an invisible rubber was erasing all trace of him, starting with the rim working round and down until there was nothing left but emptiness and silence.

The joy they felt at the eradication of their enemy was tempered by the tragic loss of Balgaire. Tiblou sat quietly holding his friend, rocking back and forth. Violet hovered beside them, wand pointing to the ground, her wings affected by the sadness, dull and limp. Neve drifted over to them and rested a hand on Tibs' shoulder. "He was a wonderful man, an even greater wizard and none of us will ever forget him." She leant forwards and gently prised him away from Balgaire. Then Roger and Chet carried the wizard's lifeless body back to the café, followed by the others who walked in a line in silence, their heads bowed and tears flowing down their cheeks.

CHAPTER SEVENTEEN

There was no time to grieve further for Balgaire. His successor had to be found immediately. Tradition demanded that Sherwood must always have a wizard and so a replacement needed to be named as soon as possible.

The procession had only just got back to the café when a shimmering ball appeared in the air in front of the door. The sphere turned out to be a roll of parchment which unfolded and a floating pen began to write on it. It spelt out T. I .B .L .O .U. in large old-fashioned letters,

"This *can't* be right!" exclaimed Tibs. "Surely someone of mature years, with much more life experience, like Uncle Roger, would be a more suitable candidate. I'm far too young for such responsibility."

"There is some logic to it," said Annie, giving him a motherly smile. Balgaire always took a great interest in you and encouraged everything you did."

"But it's too much. I don't know enough. I don't know *anything*. I really don't want to inherit Balgaire's mantle."

Neve stepped forward. "It's about to happen, Tiblou, whether you like it or not. I've known for a long time that he intended you to be his successor. Balgaire was only too aware the battle with Mordrog could end the way it did and so he'd begun preparing for it. Hence... you, Tibs."

As if to confirm this decision in everyone's mind, the scroll began to fill as it rolled further down. Larna peered forwards and read the names at the bottom :

'SIGNED BY (Balgaire's scribble) and WITNESSED THIS DAY (date) By: NEVE, WITCH OF SHERWOOD (Her signature began to appear) on behalf of: THE SUPREME CONSUL, GRAND

WIZARD DRYDEN (his flowery signature filled the space). A huge blob of red wax dropped onto the bottom of the parchment and was stamped with the Seal of the Ancients by an invisible hand. Then, as Larna finished reading, the whole thing curled back up and evaporated into thin air. At the same moment, Balgaire's body rose into the night sky, higher and higher. They followed his progress, mouths open in wonderment, until... a blue sphere appeared and opened to admit his lifeless form, then silently closed.

All eyes were still cast at the sky as Balgaire's robe and wand began to descend and landed at Tiblou's feet. He stepped back, too afraid to touch the robe, and then changed his mind, knelt down and scooped it up. Annie took the garment from him and handed it to Neve.

"Come on, son. It's time," she said.

Tiblou took off his long black coat, revealing his green jeans and white blousy top. Then the two women positioned themselves behind him and placed the robe over his shoulders. He staggered a little. Larna wondered whether this was from the weight of the material or from the weight of his new responsibilities. As his arms went into the sleeves, it shrank to his size. The stains from Balgaire's blood faded and the holes made by the tree branch began to weave together. On Tiblou the garment was pristine. Then, as he pulled himself up to his full height, the most miraculous thing of all took place. All trace of Tibs' canine features slowly disappeared until he resembled a typical teenager.

"Your tail has gone." Chet commented pushing his way through the crowd. Tiblou twisted at the waist, nearly falling over trying to see his rear. "You're right, it's vanished." He suddenly laughed. "Can't say I'll miss it one bit, always getting in the way." Abashed, he looked at his mother's tail, "Sorry, mum, that was insensitive, totally out of order." Annie smiled and patted his shoulder. "Don't be silly, son, you're allowed a few mistakes to begin with." She and Chet exchanged glances. "We're absolutely thrilled for you, aren't we?" she beamed, nudging her other son in the ribs.

"Of course we are. Anyway, I'm rather attached to my tail, brother."

Everyone took that as their cue to rush forward, crowd round Tibs and inspect his new physical state. There was a tremendous racket, people firing off questions and not waiting for answers. Larna and Aron were in the middle of it all, their faces shining. It was easily the happiest moment they had experienced since arriving in this strange future world.

* * *

The surprises weren't yet over. The past was still making way for the future. Neve raised both arms skyward and closed her eyes. She stood there, still and quiet. Her lips moved but there was no sound. Seconds later, a transformation began to take place. Neve's hair gradually tidied itself whilst her dress became whole, fresh and clean again. Likewise with Violet. All traces of the conflict with Mordrog had been extinguished. Then the old woman picked up Balgaire's wand and held it out in front of her. It split in two. One half grew into another full-size wand and the second half became his staff. Neve lowered her arms and walked slowly towards Tiblou.

The significance of the occasion was not lost on Tibs. He stood to attention and seemed taller. As if instinct told him that this was *the* moment when he officially took on the persona of a wizard. There would be no going back to being 'ordinary Tiblou'. His life from now on would never be the same. So many would be reliant on him.

Chet and their Uncle Roger stood either side of him, his mother, Annie, behind. The crowd had swelled with the news, waiting, and for the first time in a long time, they felt at ease. No more darting glances, looking for the 'evil eye' watching everything they did. The atmosphere was joyous as a sense of peace settled on them all.

Aron and Larna watched with pride and fascination as their grandmother solemnly placed the wand in Tiblou's right hand and the staff in his left. There was complete silence for quite a while. Then, taking three steps back, she gave a slight nod to Violet who flew in front of Tibs at eye-level and waved her wand. A large golden picture frame materialised containing a blank canvas, which Larna suspected was the one she'd seen in the portrait gallery under Balgaire's house. It stood beside the young wizard-elect, as if waiting. The ancient robe that Tiblou was wearing changed again, and when the transformation was complete, he stood resplendent in his own emerald green ceremonial garment. He smiled at Violet and patted his right shoulder with the crystal-topped staff. She accepted and settled herself comfortably, legs crossed at the ankles. Finally, the staff and wand morphed back into one, now emerald green to match the robe. Within seconds the canvas came to life, as if someone were painting a picture in oils. The finished portrait was breath taking and a true likeness of them both. Tiblou then stuffed the wand deep inside one of his voluminous pockets. The instalment of the new wizard was complete. A loud cheer went up from the crowd, Larna and Aron joining in at the top of their voices, belting it out with the best of them.

"Now I believe we have unfinished business," said Tibs.

The young wizard turned to the youngsters and spoke with a new authority. "We ought to pick up where Balgaire left off, regarding your blood, and hopefully find a cure. I've noticed more and more people are changing, so it won't be much longer before everyone reaches the point of no return."

Aron and Larna were as keen as Tibs to give their much-needed blood. They desperately wanted to help their friends who were suffering so badly and with whom they now felt such a strong bond. They also wanted it all to be over, to go home with Neve and relax in her cottage in the forest after all the terrors they'd endured. It seemed a simple and perfect end to an amazing adventure. But it was not to be. A new enemy would see to that!

CHAPTER EIGHTEEN

Tiblou led the way into the forest, the others surrounding Larna and Aron like body guards. Neve walked one side, Annie the other while Chet brought up the rear and Violet hovered overhead like a scout. Nothing untoward happened except that Larna and Aron managed to trip up several times and felt angry with themselves for their new-found clumsiness. There was no sign of Edsel anywhere, so it couldn't be his doing... or could it?

Before long, they found themselves approaching Tiblou's house. Instead of the quirky little cottage that once stood there, there was now a much larger building. Made of red brick, it had two turrets, one at each end of a grey slate roof. It was two storeys high with square white-framed windows on both floors enclosed by oak shutters. A broad smile played on Tiblou's lips as he gave a satisfied nod of approval to his new home. It was totally different from Balgaire's, but equally as extraordinary.

As they walked through the gate, Larna hurried over and peering in through one of the windows. "This place is awesome," she said. "You're going to love living here, Tibs."

"Do you think you'll have one of those fish-tank rooms, like the one at Balgaire's?" Aron wanted to know.

"I might." He laughed. "I wish you could have seen your faces when I pushed your hand inside that tank. Perhaps I'll be able to conjure it up one day especially for you, once I know how to control my new powers. That's if you ever decide to come back for a visit."

Aron was curious to know. "If you can do that, why not bring Balgaire back?"

Tiblou sighed. "I wish. Even Violet's amazing healing powers only managed to do that for a few minutes. Just long enough to distract Mordrog... ”

Aron cut in and drew a line across his throat, “So Yaya could polish him off!”

“That's right, but even Neve, the Great White Witch, can only do so much.” He looked around. “That's odd, I wonder where she is. She was just behind us a minute ago. Come to think of it, where's Violet?”

He pushed open the plain white front door and went inside. Chet and Annie were already inside, having gone on ahead, but not the other two. Larna and Aron dashed from room to room, calling their names, but there was no reply. Back at the front door they met up with Tibs again. Everyone looked worried.

“Where's Yaya?”

“I honestly don't know, Larna. We need to find her and Violet quickly.” Tibs pressed the heels of his hands to his head. “My senses are telling me that something is wrong. Very wrong.”

“Right, where do we start?” Aron tried to roll up his sleeves as if he wanted a fight with someone.

“At the moment I haven't a clue.” He touched his temples and closed his eyes. “I need to go into a trance like Balgaire did when we were looking for you, Aron. And I feel we need to be back in the garden. Don't ask me why.”

They followed Tibs outside and stood in the middle of the front garden, waiting anxiously. “Form a circle so I can stand in the middle,” he instructed. “And please be patient. This is my very first challenge and I want to make sure I get it right.” He raised his arms and waited. Eyes closed, perfectly still. Everyone watched quietly as a blue mist slowly descended and surrounded him. The eerie silence was eventually broken when Tibs cried out, *“OH, NO!”*

“What is it, dear? What have you seen?” gasped Annie.

“Neve and Violet are in a dreadful place, but I've no idea where it is or how they got there.” He staggered and put out a hand to steady himself. Chet caught him just in time. “I don't understand,” said Chet. “With Mordrog gone, there's nobody left who'd want to harm us.”

"I have a terrible feeling there *is* someone, bro. Think about it for a minute. Who stole Mordrog's wand ? Who stands to gain a fortune by taking over the warlock's cruel scheme? Who enjoys being evil for its own sake?"

"Edsel!" they all exclaimed together.

Annie took her son by the elbows and shook him gently, making him look her in the eyes. "Are you saying Neve and Violet could be in mortal danger?"

Tiblou nodded miserably. "Yes I am. If the darkness overtakes them, we'll never see either of them again." He gulped. "I wish Balgaire were still here. I didn't want this so soon... "

"Stop it!" said Annie, sharply. "Nobody's blessed with instant wisdom, and whatever else, it takes time." She tapped his cheek. "Have a little faith in the ability and skill you have gained already and start again." She drew a slow breath. "See if you can picture where they are. Let's all hold hands and concentrate really hard, and see what happens. Yes?"

Forming another circle round Tiblou, the group joined hands and closed their eyes. Immediately, Larna began to feel hot and light-headed. Instinct told her to pull her hands free, but they felt glued to Chet's on her right and Aron's on her left. Then she felt a strong mental pull towards a wall of blackness. Of dread and despair. She'd never experienced anything like it before in her life and hoped she never would do so again. Yelling out, her eyes shot open. The spell broke and they all shook and blew on their burning hands.

Annie was white-faced. Aron was shaking uncontrollably.

Tiblou was about to collapse, so Chet slung his arms around him and held him upright. Everyone looked frightened.

"Oh, Yaya, what's happened to you?" wailed Larna.

"They're in the Forest of Darkness aren't they, Tibs?" said Annie, cooly.

"Yes," replied Tibs, nodding his head grimly. "They're prisoners there."

"How did this happen?" Aron's forehead was crinkled into a deep frown.

"Somehow, Neve and Violet have been spirited to this dreadful place which is connected to the Dark Side of our world," explained Annie. "We have to find them before they pass through the Realm of the Shadows and enter Eternal Darkness."

"And if we can't?" Larna whispered, her heart thudding because she realised she knew the answer already. Annie, Chet and Tibs looked knowingly at each other and for a few seconds nobody spoke.

Annie was first to break the silence. "We mustn't give up. We must get them back. We *will* get them back. I pr... "

"DON'T MAKE PROMISES YOU CAN'T KEEP!" Aron shouted. "We might have stood a chance before, when Balgaire was here – if he hadn't gone and got himself killed. Tiblou doesn't even know how to use his powers yet, so *he's* not going to be much use, is he?"

There was a shocked silence. Larna was particularly upset. She'd never known her brother panic like that before. He was usually the casual one. "*Stop it,* Aron," she said firmly. "We're all scared and this isn't helping anybody... " She paused as the heavens opened and they were caught in torrential rainfall. They'd been so engrossed in the disappearance of Neve and Violet that they'd forgotten it was time for the daily downpour.

Soaked to the skin, Annie shooed everyone indoors. Then Tibs hit a button on the wall and said, *"DRY!"* Instantly a warm gentle breeze filled the room, fluttering their clothes. They stood in their own puddles and watched each other dry out. The rain stopped exactly on schedule, but it was getting dark outside. So Annie suggested they stayed the night and regroup in the morning. Light-headed, hungry and mentally exhausted, Aron and Larna agreed. But until they'd found their grandmother, they weren't going to be able to relax anywhere.

CHAPTER NINETEEN

Tibs somehow conjured up food to suit everybody, which Larna and Aron hardly touched except to move round the plate and back again. Their mood was sombre and, as they couldn't think of anything constructive to say, there was silence. Eventually Annie announced they needed to sleep on it and see what might turn up in the morning.

The two of them shared a bedroom similar to the one Larna had back at their grandmother's. The reminder of her pushed her further into despair. Lying on her back in the dark, tired out but unable to sleep, Larna wondered where her grandmother had got to and if she would be all right.

"Oh, Yaya!" she sighed out loud, bashing her pillow in frustration.

Aron sat up, pushed his bedding back and sat cross-legged like a mystic. "I can't sleep either, sis."

"We must try, said Larna, realising her worrying was doing neither of them any good. "If we don't get some sleep, we won't be any good tomorrow. G'night, Aron." Her brother pulled the covers over him and replied with a grunt.

From the glow of the night light Larna could just make out the wall paintings and, as she focused on them, she thought she saw the characters move. It was too dark to recognise anybody, even though she squinted, and then it all began to swim. She told herself not to be stupid. They're only paintings. But they drew her in until she felt compelled to follow the procession slowly and silently winding through the trees towards the blank fourth wall. She watched, mesmerised, as the cloaked figures crossed over onto the Dark Side. Their silvery outlines wound their way further and further into the centre of the wall, leaving a trail which glowed in the dark, like a slug. The line halted and formed a circle. The light from their outlines illuminated a grossly misshapen and stunted tree. The moment was sinister. Then the whole picture vanished, except for a very thin silvery trail.

Larna shot up, hot and sweating, though her skin felt cold. She switched on her bedside lamp. Aron was on his side with the bedding over his head, but she could tell by his breathing that he wasn't asleep. Jumping out of bed Larna went over to him and shook his shoulder.

"Aron, Aron!" she whispered, excitedly. "I think Yaya has sent us a message."

"Whaddya mean?"

Pulling the duvet back and grabbing his arm, Larna pulled her brother out of bed and took him to the wall. "Look!" she urged.

"At what? It's a blank wall." He shook Larna off and turned back to bed.

Angry and frustrated, Larna seized Aron's pyjama jacket, nearly pulling it off and thrust his face to the wall.

"Humour me, brother. Come closer and have a really good look. Now, what can you see?" Nose almost touching, Aron peered hard and then looked back at Larna who was nodding enthusiastically. He peered again, shaking his head in disgust. Twisting round Larna was dismayed to find she couldn't see anything either. Deeply disappointed she let Aron go back to bed and slowly climbed into her own.

"Put the light out. We're supposed to be getting some shut-eye." Aron grumbled.

"Sorry."

"I bet you were dreaming. Go to sleep." With that he turned away and pulled the covers back over his head.

In that instant all Larna's excitement turned to misery. Leaning over she switched off the light, bashed the pillows again and snuggled down. But sleep wouldn't come. She tossed and turned. As a last resort, she tried to empty her head of all thoughts, a little trick her mum had taught her. It worked. She began to drift. In a semi-conscious state, she began counting the light pulses showing through her eyelids. She managed eight before realisation dawned. There shouldn't be any light signals! She opened both eyes and stared at the blank wall.

"Look at this, Aron!" she exclaimed. "Wake up. Wake UP!"

"What is it this time?" he groused.

Larna could only point and stare. With bad grace Aron turned his head. Then did a double-take.

"You're right!" he gasped. "There *is* something!" Flinging aside his duvet, he sat on the edge of the bed. Together they watched the glow slowly beat its way along the same path the cloaked figures had trudged earlier until it arrived at the twisted tree. It pulsed for a few seconds on the spot, then slowly did a circular tour of the trunk. The light vanished, then after a few more seconds, it did the same thing again. They were so excited, it took all their willpower not to shout out loud. Instead they gave each other high-fives.

"That's Yaya's all right," laughed Larna. "I *know* it is! She's sent a message telling us how to find her... and Violet."

"What shall we do, Larna?"

"We've got to wake the others and tell them."

Hurrying to the door, Larna switched on all the lights to illuminate the bit of corridor outside their bedroom and they headed for the stairs. They had to pass several doors leading off the landing and tapped on each one. There was no response from any of them. Continuing along the passage, they found themselves back at their own room. Somehow they'd missed the staircase in the dark, so they set off in the other direction. The same thing happened again. They'd been round it twice and they still couldn't find the stairs.

"We can't keep going round and round in circles, Larna," cried Aron. "How are we going to find where they are?"

"Maybe we should shout. What do you think?"

Aron nodded. So they stood in the corridor and yelled at the top of their voices. They waited several seconds for someone to appear, then shouted again. No answer from Tibs or any of the others. Absolute silence.

"What are we going to do?" cried Larna, starting to panic. "We can't make anyone hear us and we don't seem to be able to find a way out... "

Aron pointed to a nearby window. "Why don't we give this a try, eh? It can't be that much of a drop, can it? I mean, it didn't look very high to me from the outside."

It took him ten seconds to push the window up. It was an old-fashioned one with ropes and pulleys either side. Poking his head out into the blackness of the night, he said. "There's one of those creeper trees on the wall, that'll make it easier." Sitting on the sill he started to swing his legs over the edge.

"Hang on a minute," called Larna, ever the sensible one. "I think we should leave a note." Rummaging in the bedside cabinet she found a pen and paper and began to write. "Hurry up," urged Aron. "I'm getting cramp and its cold out here."

Having explained where they were going and why, Larna took a couple of green tartan dressing-gowns from the open closet and put one on. She threw the other across to her brother. "Here, wear this. I'll bring our trainers." Then, one after the other, they climbed down the thick creeper with ease. Soon they were standing on firm ground.

"Come on," called Larna.

They headed off into the unknown. This time, though, they were completely on their own.

CHAPTER TWENTY

After the brightness in their bedroom, they had to stand still for a few seconds letting their eyes get accustomed to the dark, and to get their bearings. There was just enough moonlight to enable them to find their way into the forest. Once inside, though, it was a whole different ball game. The trees looked like sinister beings, full of menace, having a life of their own with each gust of wind. Larna and Aron stuck together, kept their heads down looking for a sign – anything – that would lead them in the right direction.

They walked around for ages like a couple of lost souls and were just about to give up in despair when Aron spotted something in the distance. A pure white object which shone in the darkness.

"What's that?" he queried. They ran to the spot, disappointed to find it was only a crumpled piece of paper. He picked it up and his eyes rounded in shock and he flapped his right hand madly, trying to shake the paper off.

"It burnt me!" he cried in disbelief, holding out his hand palm-up. "Look!" Sure enough, there were burns on his fingers.

"What the... ?" Larna bent down to get a closer look at the object. There were scorch marks on the paper too, a perfect set of Aron's fingertips. Grabbing her brother's hand, Larna saw that the ends of his fingers had gone smooth. What sort of trick was this, burning off someone's fingerprints? She was beginning to get a bad feeling about all this and wondered whether she'd completely misread the message on the wall. Looking up into the distance she could see more luminous white scraps of paper.

In spite of their misgivings they decided to carry on following the paper trail, though they weren't tempted to pick any of them up this time. The deeper they went, the darker and more menacing the forest became. Aron, normally the brave one, held onto Larna's sleeve, maintaining he didn't want them to get separated rather than admit he was petrified. The trail was becoming more difficult underfoot and the forest seemed to be hemming them in. They had to duck under low branches, and foliage constantly bashed them in the face. Wind whipped up and they were getting cold.

The stunted tree in the wall picture was instantly recognisable, ugly and misshapen with bits of white paper round its roots. Neither of them wanted to go anywhere near it, but they knew they had to brave it to find the next clue, if any. Out of the darkness above, a large sheet of black paper materialised and snagged onto the end of one of the higher branches, but they weren't close enough to reach it or read anything that was written on it. Nervously, they inched nearer. Suddenly, bold silver letters began to appear and Larna spelled them out loud.

"S-A-Y G-O-O-D-B-Y-E." She paused to let this sink in, then squealed... "Oh *NO!*" as the penny dropped.

There wasn't enough time to call out a warning to Aron, who was right behind her, nor run away because the earth began to shake. Aron swayed and fell out of sight as Larna made a grab for the tree and missed. Then the ground opened up beneath her feet and took her down.

* * *

Falling downwards into the hole, Larna plunged feet-first into deep icy water. The shock took her breath away and made her feel numb. Needing to breathe, she fought her way upwards, taking great gulps of cold moist air as soon as her head broke the surface. Treading water, she looked around to get her bearings and was amazed to find it wasn't dark at all. There was a mellow glow, enough for Larna to see she was in a massive cave with a lake in the middle.

She swam towards some rocks where the water looked shallow. With both feet planted firmly on what felt like a grassy bed, she walked easily between the stones onto a sandy beach and looked around for Aron. The last confused memory she had of her brother was of him throwing his arms up and falling into the opening ground. Diving back into the freezing water, Larna searched in vain. There was no sight or sound of another living soul. She swam to the rocks again and wearily heaved herself up to sit on top of one of them, reasoning that Aron must have dropped through somewhere else. Sitting with her knees tucked under her chin, shivering uncontrollably, she felt more frightened and miserable than at any other time during this strange and surreal adventure in which she was involved. She was lost, alone and in danger of dying of cold. Getting up and moving around to try to get her circulation going, she suddenly felt a blast of warm air accompanied by a stench of sulphur. Following her nose, she stumbled along the tiny beach until she found a pit full of bubbling lava – the outer edge of an underground volcano. The stench of sulphur made her retch, but it was warm there, suffocatingly hot if she got too close. So she just stood there, basking in the heat, until she was dry again. It made her feel sleepy, but she knew she could not rest. She had to find Aron!

Pulling her now stiff dressing-gown together and refastening the belt, Larna stood up and looked round. There was enough light to see that there were tunnels in the rock face and she wondered what lurked down those pitch-black corridors. This time a shiver of terror ran through her body. She realised she would have to explore these tunnels. She could not climb up the way she'd come in, so they were the only way out. Trying to be brave and make light of her desperate situation, she chanted, "Eeny meeny miney mo... *that* one!" and pointed to the nearest. A dozen strides took her there and she gave a loud sigh. "Wish me luck!" Her echo repeated and repeated. It felt good to hear another voice, even if it was only her own returning to her.

It was dark inside, so Larna put out a hand to feel the way, touching damp walls as she moved. They began to glow where she'd touched. Jumping back, she pulled her hand away and yelled in surprise. Immediately, the light dimmed and went out again.

"Wow! That's so cool!" Hand over hand, she went deeper into the tunnel lighting her way as she went. It took her nowhere. Emerging from the other end, she found herself back in the cavern again. "Never mind," she said out loud. "Seven more to go."

By the fourth she was getting a bit fed-up. The fifth passage seemed to go on forever until the final bend, when she found herself once again back where she'd started in the massive cave. Frustrated, she called out, *"ARRGH... "* and heard it echo round the walls like the cries of a hundred dying men. This time she sat by the water's edge and began to worry. What if she couldn't find a way out? What if she was stuck here without food or anything forever? Apart from Aron, nobody knew where she was. What if she was never..? She shuddered and chose to cut this last thought short. Frightening herself was becoming a full-time hobby.

"Come on, Larna," she said to herself, "think positive. Get up and do something. Try another tunnel. Keep at it until you find a way out. Come on, get moving!"

Instead of heading for the sixth, she thought she'd explore the eighth and work in reverse order if that proved to be another dead end. Once again trudging across the grey sand and entering the pitch black hole, she felt her way along the tunnel wall. As before, the rock face lit her way then dimmed as she moved on. Progress was slow, but after a while she stopped and cocked an ear. She thought she'd heard a noise ahead. No, just silence. A bit further on she stopped and listened again. This time she was positive. It sounded like a soft moan, muffled and far away.

"Aron!" she called excitedly. "Is that you?"

Hand-over-hand on the wall she made her way down the tunnel as fast as she could. The voice she'd heard sounded racked with pain and this urged her on. She fell and hurt her knees but hardly felt a thing, getting up and carrying on. The poor light and the uneven floor slowed her down to almost a snail's pace. She didn't seem to be getting anywhere, no matter how fast she tried to run. Calling words of encouragement to the distant voice didn't bring a response other than the cries of pain getting louder. Hearing them, Larna really began to panic.

She came to a dead stop. Keeping both hands pressed hard

against the wall lit an area big enough for her to see that the roof had caved in. Large stones blocked the way and rumbles sounding down the passage made her fear for her brother's life.

"I'm here, Aron! Hold on!" she shouted. Somehow she found enough strength to heave some rocks out of the way, but with her hands off the wall, she was forced to work in darkness. The moans became less frequent and Larna began to worry she might be too late after all.

"Stay with me, do you hear? Don't you dare die on me!"

With renewed energy she heaved a massive boulder away leaving a gap big enough for her to see inside. But it was too dark.

Shoving her right arm into the hole and with her cheek squashed against the stones, she felt around and grabbed hold of something. It felt very cold, very clammy and was very still. Now with her adrenalin working to the max, Larna continued to move the rocks at a faster pace. She made an opening big enough to crawl into. There wasn't a sound from inside now, so she forced herself through the entrance, putting her arms out in front like a blind man and feeling for the sides. Nothing but cold stone. Then something moved, running lightly over her face, head and upper body.

"Is that you, Aron?" she gasped.
No answer from the hunched figure in front of her.

"It's not you, is it?" She was speaking her thoughts out loud. "If you were my brother, you'd know me. So who are you?"

Still no answer from the darkness. Then a whispery voice said, "Help me,"

Before Larna could say anything else, there was a crack and rumbling further down the tunnel. "We've got to get out of here before there's another cave-in." she said, trying not to sound too anxious. "Come on, help me get you out." Moving backwards on all fours was slow and painful. It must have been several minutes before she squeezed out of the prison. Leaning in again she took hold of the stranger's ankles and gave a gentle tug. There was very little movement and Larna realised she would have to pull much harder.

"Come on," she urged. "We've got to hurry. I think the roof's about to cave in." Larna was frightened they wouldn't make it out of the tunnel in time, and heaved with all the strength she had left. The trapped creature shot out like a bullet, knocking Larna over onto her back and landing on top of her. They automatically embraced and she found herself staring into the eyes of a handsome young man. They lay there for a few seconds until there was another loud crack and dust filtered through the rocks.

"We've got to move *now!*" yelled Larna.

Scrambling to her feet and hoisting his dead weight up in a fireman's lift, she ran as fast as she could away from the noise. Dust tickled the back of her throat and she began to cough. "Touch the wall, then I'll be able to see where we're going." she shouted above the deafening sound of collapsing rocks. It took a few seconds for her meaning to register before a slender outstretched hand began to light the way. It was enough for Larna to dodge the obstacles she'd tripped over on the way in. A quick glance over her other shoulder prompted another burst of energy. The roof was giving way, falling faster than she'd anticipated and catching up with them.

Larna ran for her life. She felt unreal, as if she was in a film or having one of her strange dreams again. But the danger behind her was very real and she pushed herself to the limit, the burden on her shoulders seeming to get heavier and heavier with every step. Eventually, she could run no further and sank to her knees, lowering her companion gently to the ground in the darkness.

"Can't take any more!" she wheezed, although another menacing rumble made it clear there was no time to rest.

"Go," the disembodied voice whispered.

"What?" she gasped.

"You... GO!" insisted the breathy voice.

"No. Not without you," insisted Larna. Another fall of rock behind them made her jump to her feet. "Come on. There's no time to lose!" Taking hold of an arm and a leg, she slung the mysterious being over her shoulder for the second time and headed off down the tunnel again. She was just in time to save them both from a massive roof cave-in which dropped exactly where they'd been sitting a moment before. There was nothing left of the tunnel behind and Larna feared that if they didn't get a move on, it would happen on top or in front of them as well.

Larna coaxed and cajoled, encouraging her injured companion to help as much as possible. Then the entrance to the tunnel came in sight with the underground lake beyond. "Not far now," she called, sensing the body on her shoulders weakening even further. "Come on, keep going. We're nearly there!" Hearing a clicking sound above their heads, Larna looked up. The roof cracked open, the walls shook and huge pieces of rock began to fall. It was pure instinct that made Larna fling her burden out of the tunnel and dive head-first after him.

For a few seconds after the cave-in was complete, Larna felt nothing as she watched the shadowy figure she'd rescued roll towards the water's edge and crawl in. The dust was choking. She covered her mouth and half closed her eyes in an attempt to breathe and see. The dim silhouette went under the water. Larna waited and waited, but never saw him resurface. She tried to crawl toward the lake as well but found she couldn't move. That was when she realised her legs were trapped under a mountain of rocks. That was also when she experienced the worst pain of her life... and fainted.

Sometime later, she felt something being put to her lips and heard a voice telling her to drink. Whatever it was, was sweet and tasted of herbs. After that... nothing.

CHAPTER TWENTY-ONE

It was the pain that finally woke her. She opened her eyes to somebody wiping her forehead. They put their other hand on her shoulder and said slowly, "Not move, please." The voice was soft and gentle.

"What's going on?" asked Larna. She was stretched out on the water's edge, her head on a cushion. From behind, cool hands held either side of her head.

"You have accident... we put you back together," the gentle voice said haltingly.

"Where's Aron?"

"Aron?"

"My brother. I was looking for him."

"No Aron. Only you and me."

"Who are you?"

"My name is Cai. You rescued me."

"Am I dreaming this?"

"No, this is real. You badly injured. Need looking after."

Alarm bells started ringing in her head and she struggled to see who was talking. Firm hands held her still. Her legs felt hot and a powerful stinging sensation worked its way from her toes upwards. Looking down she was shocked to see some form of splint on her left leg. The other seemed bent. Struggling to sit up, Larna turned to get a glimpse of her softly-spoken companion. He was a boy of about her own age, slightly shorter than her. He had long golden brown wavy hair tied back from a broad forehead. His eyes were of the deepest blue with eyebrows that tipped up a little at the outer edges. His nose was straight and shapely with a firm-looking mouth underneath. He wore a figure-hugging dark green outfit that looked like a diver's wet-suit and no shoes. Most striking of all, however, was his dazzling smile. It lit up his pale green, slightly luminous skin like the sun. Larna felt an electric shock arc between the two of them and nearly jumped out of her skin. Their eyes met. He was smiling. He had a beautiful smile.

"You save Cai... now Cai save you," he said simply, pointing across at the caved-in tunnel.

Larna's memory suddenly returned and she shuddered to think what nearly happened to them. She wanted to thank the young man but needed to be face-to-face to do it. Turning slightly she realised her head had been cradled in his lap, not on a cushion.

"Where's my brother?"

"No brother. Only me."

"You couldn't have moved those rocks, Cai, unless you had some help."

"My father called his... what you say... workers? Soldiers? They free you just in time."

Cai helped to push from behind as Larna manoeuvred herself upright. Having a leg in splints was not only uncomfortable but every movement was awkward. Larna realised the pain she'd felt before had faded away and made a mental note to ask what Cai had done when she was unconscious. It must have been a powerful drug with miraculous healing powers.

The water in the lake looked inviting. Larna was desperate to have a good wash. She felt dirty and dishevelled after their ordeal and thinking of water reminded her, she was desperate for a drink. She was just scooping some of the cool water into her mouth when a breathy twittering sounded from across the lake. Cai answered in the same way.

"What was that?" Larna asked anxiously.

"My father want to know if you well enough for a visit. Told him yes and he will come to us now." He noted Larna's look of surprise. "It only right that he come and... and give you his thanks."

"For what?"

"My life. Said before – you gave me back my life."

Cai helped Larna to sit on a flat rock close to the lake. Then he fetched her some water in a large shell and held it while she splashed her hands and face. She felt better after that.

"My father is here."

"Where?" Larna couldn't see or hear him.

"He not come with any fuss."

"Pardon?"

Suddenly, millions of little dots of light lit the cavern and twinkled like static stars attached to the roof. Cai noticed Larna's look of amazement and smiled. "They are harmless little creatures that live up there. They are our friends and give us light when we need it."

"Wow!" She was gobsmacked again. "What are they called?"

"Lumins." He moved closer to Larna. "Now watch the water," he whispered.

There was a silence for a few seconds until an elderly green man rose from the water in a stately manner. Head held high, steely grey long hair, he walked in a straight-backed manner on his long legs. His unusual robe was of royal blue with gold trim. And his vivid blue eyes startled Larna, as if they looked deep into her head and knew what she was thinking. Not knowing what to do or say, Larna left first contact to Cai. The young man stood silently in front of his father and bowed his head. They talked fast until the old man looked over the boy's shoulder at Larna.

"So, you are the one who saved my son," he stated. "As you cannot come to me, I will come to you. Do not worry about your legs, they will mend very quickly. Cai and his mother, Darla, have repaired you as much as they are able. They gave you one of their special healing potions. It also takes away the pain and discomfort."

Cai led his father from the water's edge. Both stood in front of Larna, took her hands and gently pulled her to her feet. Looking down at her legs, she was surprised not to feel any discomfort at all. "We not able to straighten your leg, but you not be harmed walking on it. When you return to your own kind, they mend it for you. You never know that it and other one was damaged."

Head on one side, the King studied Larna, came to a decision and said. "Your name is Larner? Not daring to correct his pronunciation, Larna nodded dumbly. "At great risk to yourself, you saved the life of my dear and only son, earning my deepest gratitude. So I will grant you one favour, Larner. Choose wisely and choose now."

There was no hesitation in Larna's mind. She knew just what she wanted.

"Thank you, sir," she said. "Err, what is your name, by the way?"

"Drisco," answered Cai's father. "King Drisco, lord of this domain, ruler of my people, the Undines."

"Thank you, King Drisco," repeated Larna. "I've made my decision and would very much like to find my brother, Aron, and also save Yaya, my grandmother."

The King went quiet on hearing this. Drawing Cai close he said, "That is very commendable of you, Larner. The favour I grant. You wish it for others who are dear to you. That affects me deeply." He turned his head away and Larna thought she spotted tears in his eyes.

Cai took over from his father. "My grandmother, Drisco's mother, she was taken by the Dryads," he explained. "They found a way down here and... er... took away some of us. A few of my father's people were among the taken and not seen again. She cannot return. She will be no more."

"What are Dryads?" asked Larna.

"Tree people in your world. Dryads hide and become as one with the trees. We only go up to search for them during the darkness. We die in the light. It dries our skin and we just... " he couldn't finish.

Drisco gave a good imitation of a cough and said, "Come on, my son, Larner needs our help." He clapped his hands and the lake began to boil. Larna jumped back in astonishment. Out of the water marched about a dozen people. Women as well as men. All good looking, all green, and dressed entirely in green. Like Drisco, no shoes. They stood in a semicircle round Cai and his father. They were waiting for orders.

"These are my people. You saved my only child and heir. They saved you and have asked to help you find your way to the world above. My son," he gazed fondly at Cai, "wishes to go with you as far as he can." He paused. "And I have given my permission. Don't worry about your legs, Larner. Do not look down at them, they will not hurt you now."

"I... I... " Larna was lost for words.

"There is no need to say more." He reached out and shook Larna's hand. They both knew this wasn't going to be their last meeting. Then King Drisco turned, walked back into the water and disappeared below the surface.

CHAPTER TWENTY-TWO

Aron crawled to the stumpy tree only to find that the hole had closed. He had not fallen like Larna thought he had. He began to dig frantically with his bare hands.

"*LARNA. L-A-A-A-RNA...* " he screamed.

After a while he realised the faster he dug down, the quicker the hole filled up. So he was forced to give up through sheer exhaustion.

Lying with his tear-streaked cheek on the damp soil, he knew he had to make the biggest decision of his life. Continue digging in the hope of getting somewhere or leave Larna to her fate and fetch help? With one last ditch-effort he resumed digging for a while, but his fingers were so sore and bloody that he was forced to stop. In the end he decided to retrace their steps following the scraps of paper which continued to curl at the edges then burst into flames when he passed. As he ran branches scraped his face, tore at his dressing gown and his pyjama bottoms, but he didn't feel a thing. Then, to his horror, the remaining papers burst into flames and the ashes blew high into the night sky and dispersed, falling as sooty deposits. This stopped him in his tracks. Without the glow from the papers blazing a trail, he didn't know which way to go, which path to take.

Making his choice he ran on until the trees seemed to close ranks and become so dense he couldn't go any further. Nettles stung him and hawthorn cut through the thin nightwear, tearing the material to shreds. Somewhere along the way he'd lost the belt, then the dressing gown, and finally some of the buttons had been yanked off the pyjama jacket. Disorientated, he turned round looking for a path, but there wasn't one.

"Oh, Yaya, what am I to do?" he called. "I'm lost and so is

Larna. I don't believe you sent any message... " His knees buckled, dropping him to the ground. Curling up like a baby, he began to shiver violently and lay there utterly defeated.

The wind whistled through the trees and distant sounds of laughter filled his head. Leaves that had been disturbed began to settle on top of him until only his face was visible. Feeling drowsy, he couldn't keep his eyes open. Mumbling almost incoherently, "What's the point. Yaya's gone. Larna's gone. And I'm lost so what's the poin... " His body temperature dropped dangerously low as he drifted into a deep, overpowering sleep, failing to hear the voices calling his and his sister's names.

* * *

As time passed Aron began to dream. It was a bad dream in which he felt something touching him, crawling all over him. But in his semi-comatose state he believed he was shaking it off. Far-away voices entered his nightmare. He curled into a tighter ball under the blanket of leaves for warmth and protection against the creatures of the night that were chasing him. Then he dreamt his covers were being pulled off him and he began to thrash around. "Leave me alone... " he slurred through icy cold lips. "Jusss... leeve... me... loooo... "

In his mind, the evil-looking trees had formed a circle round him. Their branches poked unmercifully at him as he tried to fight them off. He felt himself being grabbed and then he dreamt he was floating and relaxed into it – whatever *it* might be.

CHAPTER TWENTY-THREE

"Now we go, Larna," said Cai. "Before we alert Boggrets. Must be in silence for a while. Come."

Larna had never heard of Boggrets – though their name sounded sinister – and was about to ask when Cai took her hand and led her down to the lake.

"Can you move in water?" he asked.

Nodding, Larna made swimming motions with her arms. "Like this?"

"Like that!" Cai turned to the nearest woman and held out his hand. He was given a box which he opened and took out a sort of mask. "Wear this and you will be well, Larna. We are going to take you deep under to a place where you will escape the Boggrets and I will take you back to the world above where your friends are. We came from up there in the beginning." He knew Larna wanted to ask lots more questions, but there was no time. "Come, we must hurry. Put on mask, practice breathing, then follow."

After a bit of a struggle, Larna pulled the mask over her head like a balaclava and took her first experimental breaths. It felt fine. Then another splint was put on her twisted leg, enabling her to swim in a crazy crawl-like fashion. They waded out into the water, followed by the green-bodied guards. By the time she'd been submerged for a few minutes, Larna had got the hang of it. Down and down they all swam towards an opening in the rock-face and through an inverted V-shaped entrance. The water was crystal clear and Larna could see Cai's slim form by her side. The others were around them in formation. As they slowed, the young prince's long hair swirled around his face and he touched Larna's arm, indicating that she should tread water. She nodded and Cai shot upwards with half the guards, the others staying close to

Larna. Eventually Cai returned and beckoned her to follow him. The others looked at each other anxiously. Then everyone moved off again, swimming in formation until they reached a solid wall of rock. Pointing downwards, Cai mimed that this was the direction they should take. Larna guessed he must have spotted danger above and had decided to go the long way round which definitely wasn't the scenic route.

It would have been pitch black and very claustrophobic so deep down if Cai and the guards hadn't switched on the lights attached to their belts, powerful enough to shine several feet in front of them. Beyond the beams, everything looked dark and threatening as they glided towards a fissure in the rock face. The mask magnified the fish creatures that swam threateningly towards them. Larna was momentarily afraid until the guards waved the fish on their way. Then Cai pointed and they followed him through the narrow crack. On the other side, he indicated that they were going up. Larna was very tired now, being handicapped by her injured legs. The guards on either side realised she was experiencing some difficulty and joined hands for her to sit on. A third swam behind and helped. They rose slowly, Cai in the lead until they reached just below the surface. He turned, put a finger over his lips and blew a few bubbles, indicating for them to stay quiet. As one, they switched off their lamps, plunging everything into inky blackness.

In the darkness, Larna thought of the enormity of the mission ahead of her. Finding Aron and the others, searching for Neve and Violet, giving blood to help her friends find a cure. They were formidable tasks. Her heart thumped. She raised her head and watched as Cai and some of the guards broke the surface and looked around. After a few minutes, they returned and helped Larna up and out of the water. She was carefully placed on her back at the water's edge, feeling very uncomfortable on what appeared to be sharp-edged shingle. But she was past caring because, out of the water, her legs were beginning to feel as though they belonged to her again and they were extremely painful.

Cai bent over her, helped to take off the breathing mask and adjusted the splints. "Sorry, Larna," he said. "We take the long way. Boggrets waiting for us at first exit."

"Who or what are Boggrets?" she asked at last.

Cai inclined his head to one side, thought carefully and then answered. "They evil creatures who, like us, used to live in realm above where your friends are. We Undines live there too, once, in lakes and streams and pools in the forest. We feared nothing and harmed no-one, until Boggrets discovered us and persecuted us almost to death. We took refuge down here for safety. Many lifetimes passed. We adjust to our new home and live in peace. But they find us again and move down here to continue hunting us. They led by their ruthless leader, Killian, who want to kill my father and take over his kingdom, same as they did when we lived above in the light."

"So both the worlds of the forest are threatened by evil," commented Larna. "First Mordrog and now Edsel seek to destroy the good on the surface; Killian and his Boggrets want to do the same below ground. It's all so sad."

"It is indeed... " murmured Cai, thoughtfully. Then he broke out of his reverie with a start. "We must go. Not safe here. We have good advantage over the Boggretts because they cannot swim. But they'll be running through the tunnels to catch us. If you to get back to your friends unharmed, we must be gone before they arrive."

Larna's legs were still giving her trouble and she realised there was no way she could walk anywhere under her own steam, so she was very grateful to see some of the guards twisting strange fibres into a large sling to carry her. Then one of the female guards made a twittering noise, looking eagerly around and pointing to one of the many tunnels. Immediately, two of the others wrapped each end of the sling round their wrists and nodded for Larna to sit on it. It wasn't very comfortable. She wobbled about and had to grasp their shoulders for support. They set off at a trot towards the chosen tunnel. The only light came from their belts but it was enough to see the slimy, grey uneven walls and sharp objects jutting out from either side. Some looked sharp and dangerous and would cause a lot of damage if anyone accidently scraped against them. So everyone was careful to keep in the middle.

The tunnel twisted and turned with other passages branching off at intervals. They all looked alike to Larna who was totally confused. Cai obviously knew the correct route to take and they finished by making a mad dash towards some ancient steps. "Up! Up!" he urged, waving his arms for them to hurry. "I hear Killian's foot-soldiers behind us." Larna was jostled about and reached the top in double-quick time. Cai raced on ahead holding a large, rusty key which he inserted into an ancient lock in a door in front of them. He tried to turn it. Nothing! The noise behind them was getting louder. The Boggrets were coming, marching in time and making a terrible noise. In a panic, Cai dropped the key which bounced down the steps. He ran after it. Everyone behind Larna was getting frantic, preparing for a confrontation. Cai leapt back up the steps two at a time, pushed the key back into the lock and tried again. Larna could see he wasn't strong enough, so she jumped off the sling and gently removed his hands from the key.

"Let me try," she said, turning the key with all her might and feeling something moving inside, though not enough to unlock it. "Feels as though it hasn't been used in years."

"You right, Larna. This way abandoned years ago. Too dangerous. To help you escape, we forced to use it because all other ways blocked by Killian's men."

Larna felt humbled by the help she was getting from these total strangers. They were putting themselves in great danger to help her. Their kindness was overwhelming and she said so.

"You not be silly, Larna. Of course you worthy of our help. You saved me, only son of King Drisco. Now *hurry, please*. They are but a few paces away."

Larna gave her best shot and using all her strength managed to turn the key. Rust and dirt dropped onto her feet when she pulled the key out of the lock and handed it back to Cai. The guards who'd carried her tried to push the old wooden door open and failed, so with their combined strength they shoulder-charged it. The hinges squealed in protest but didn't snap off as the door opened, a bit at a time, until it gave completely and flapped back.

Turning to let Cai go through first, Larna saw an army of creatures march into the passage. She felt petrified with fear. The guards picked her up and almost threw her outside as Killian's men mounted the steps brandishing red hot sword-like points at them. Murderous noises came from their throats and the stench from their bodies was both terrifying and nauseating. Their eyes blazed fanatically. They were grotesque.

Outside, Cai and Larna lay gasping for breath on the damp soil, willing all the guards to make it out safely. The last one quickly turned and banged the door shut. Then it was held firmly in place with the help of two more hefty Undine guards. Killian's men must have reached the other side at the same moment because they were trying to push it open. Larna could see the three Undines were struggling to keep the door shut, so more of Cai's guards pushed frantically on the wood until the key could be inserted and it was finally locked. Everyone heaved a deep sigh of relief and sank to the ground around Larna.

The danger over, Larna looked around, trying to get her bearings. It was a shock to realise they were sitting in the shadow of a huge oak tree which Cai told her was called the Major Oak. It was hollow inside. Noticing her puzzled frown, Cai chuckled, "Yes, we come up in middle of that ancient tree. It save us many times through our generations."

"How?" Larna enquired.

"The middle died centuries ago, but tree still lives on the outside. It been a friend to us for, oh, I don't know how long. I told people from your own world used to hide inside it many hundreds of years ago."

Larna started laughing. "You can't mean Robin Hood. He wasn't real!" Then she saw the look on Cai's face. "Was he?" The boy smiled, mischievously. "How do you know he was not? You always doubt stories handed down through time? Must be some truth in them to last so long. Anyway, it a mystery you will never solve and will always wonder truth of it." Cai stood up. A tinge of sadness entered his voice. "It is time we left. One of your days has gone and I know your friends very worried."

"How?"

"Now you above ground, they know where to look and will come for you."

It suddenly occurred to Larna that Cai and his guards had no safe way of returning home. The Boggrets were waiting for them. The prince read her mind. "Do not worry about us, Larna. We Undines are resourceful and can adapt to most situations. As you have probably guessed we can change shape. Besides there is water nearby in which we will be safe until Killian gets tired and goes back to his black pit."

"So long as you're sure, Cai."

"I am sure." He opened a pouch attached to his belt and brought out a disc. "King Drisco gave me this for you, Larna. Long ago, it was precious to one who lives above the ground. My father wishes you to accept it with our gratitude and said your friends will know what it means. Also, Drisco states that you are always welcome in our world down here."

With shaky hands, Larna took the round object and clasped it to her chest. This was a parting Larna was dreading. Even though she'd only known him for a few hours, she felt sick at the thought of leaving Cai.

"Can't you stay a bit longer?"

He shook his head. "It is time to say... " He looked directly into her eyes "... maybe we meet again. Who knows, if you start to believe in Robin Hood, you will believe in dreams – and me."

Tears prickled behind Larna's eyes, but she fought them back. Cai came close to her and held her hands. Then he leaned in until their foreheads touched. "Close your eyes, Larna, and think only of your friends. They detect where you are. Keep them shut very tight and do not open them."

* * *

When she eventually opened her eyes again, she was alone. She saw several glistening trails and one sparkling set of foot prints that had slipped into the trees and vanished.

CHAPTER TWENTY-FOUR

The sun came up and Larna began to feel drowsy in the heat. With two duff legs, she couldn't go wandering off into the forest, so she leaned back against the Major Oak and closed her eyes. She began to drift, dreaming of Cai with his slim body and dazzling smile. A hand shaking her shoulder woke her abruptly.

"At last, Larna!" said Tiblou. "What happened to you and Aron?"

"We went to look for Yaya and Violet. There was a 'goodbye' message on a tree and I fell through the earth into another world. I thought he'd fallen with me, but I couldn't find him so I must have left him behind."

"That's similar to what he said."

"You've *found* him?" whooped Larna, joy coursing through the whole of her body.

"Yes. Once we'd taken him home and medicated him, he was almost back to normal."

"What else did he tell you?"

"That the two of you were following clues to trace Neve and Violet."

"Yes, yes, that's what we thought, but I don't think she sent the messages."

"No, she can't have, but somebody did. Somebody who wants you two out of the way for good. And they very nearly succeeded, too!"

He sat on the ground next to Larna and ran his hands up and down her splinted legs. "Hmm. You can tell us about this when we get you back." He picked up the tattered hem of Larna's dressing gown. "Your clothes are almost as torn and dirty as your brother's. They'll all have to be burnt."

Then Chet arrived dragging what resembled a kid's cart. The heat seemed to be getting to him because Larna could see sweat glistening on his forehead and upper lip. "Come on, hurry up," he called. "We've still got to find Neve and Violet before it's too late. And we're going to have to get there the old-fashioned way."

It was a while before they managed to position Larna comfortably on the cart. Tibs pulled and Chet pushed her along the uneven paths and across clearings until they saw Tiblou's handsome red-brick house in the distance. Annie opened the door for them and looked shocked at the state of Larna's legs sticking out in front of her. Before she could ask any questions, Larna said, "I'll tell you all about it later, Annie. How's Aron?"

"Not bad, considering he was suffering from hypothermia. I expect you'll be hungry."

"And thirsty." Larna was so relieved that Aron was safe and she was back with her friends that she said the first thing that entered her head. "I'll eat anything and everything except roast Boggret. Evil, smelly little creatures. They tried to kill me. And Cai."

The others were horrified. They sat Larna down in a comfy armchair.

"Boggrets?" gasped Tiblou, his eyes and mouth rounded. "You've met the *Boggrets*? And they let you go... ?"

Annie produced some sandwiches and a warm drink which Larna stuffed into her mouth immediately. "Actually, they chased us but we got away," she said, talking with her mouth full and almost choking.

"So who's this Cai?" asked Annie curiously.

"He's a prince," answered Larna, her eyes becoming dreamy. "I saved his life, then he saved mine."

Annie looked at Tibs and Chet, raising her eyebrows very slightly. They both hid their smiles. Then they inspected Larna's legs, nodding their approval.

"Whoever straightened your legs and splinted them up did a first class job," commented Chet. "Unfortunately, you won't be going anywhere, so you'll have to stay here while we go and search for Neve and Violet."

"NO!" shouted Larna, showering food everywhere. "You're not leaving me behind." She knew she was being irrational, but couldn't help it.

"Not possible, Larna," sighed Tibs. "You'd be a liability in your condition. He paused for a moment. "But there is a way. It might be a bit painful... "

"What is it?" she asked with renewed hope. "I don't care so long as I can go with you."

Tibs left them, returning after a few minutes carrying several pieces of metal. "Those splints have to come off and you must put these on. The difference being, your splints are full-leg, making it impossible for you to bend your knees, while these are lightweight and comprise of one set above the knee and one set below, held together by a moving knee joint which will enable you to walk. Do you understand?"

"Of course I do." She was impatient to get going. "Tibs, just do it will you, please."

Aron sauntered in, sleepy-eyed. "What's happening then?" When he saw his sister, his face lit up and widened into the biggest grin imaginable. Then he dashed over and flung his arms around her in a bear hug. "I thought we were both goners. What happ... " He looked at the others and seeing the preparations caught on immediately. "Hey, I'm alright now. If Larna's going with you in her condition, so am I." Realising Aron could be stubborn, and as he didn't look any worse for his adventure, they gave in.

Annie, Chet and Tibs got to work on Larna's legs immediately while Aron filled her in on his second near-death experience. He was just about to break into full flow when the others took hold of Larna's elbows and raised her to her feet. Tibs stepped back a few paces. "Right. See how you feel walking." She tried, wobbled dangerously and nearly fell her full length before her knees would bend. Time was passing. They needed to get a move on before the sun was at its height, so she kept practising until she felt comfortable. Walking up and down the room, she gave them a full version of her spent underground and eventual escape. Annie kept nodding, eyes getting rounder and rounder. Tiblou and Chet glanced at each other occasionally, but didn't utter a word.

When she finished, Tiblou shook his head and said, "You weren't meant to leave the house, you know. To protect you, I'd altered the corridors so nobody could get in during the night. It didn't enter my head you would climb out through the window."

"That was your idea!" exclaimed Larna, looking accusingly at her brother. "And a right mess it got us into. Didn't it?"

"How was I to know you'd go and fall down a stupid hole in the ground?" retorted Aron.

"I didn't fall! Someone got me..."

"Stop bickering, you two," snapped Chet, stepping in and taking control. "If you're intending to help us, you need to focus. We have to leave *now*."

Annie eyed Larna up and down and pulled a face. "She can't go *anywhere* in those filthy rags. Come with me." Larna followed her to the stairs and wondered how on earth she was going to climb them. She needn't have worried, though, because the first stair began to extend towards them. Helping Larna on, she twisted the acorn on top of the newel post and they rose gently to the first floor. A gap appeared in the banister rail and they stepped off into the corridor. There was no time to marvel at the intricacies of the contraption, or have a shower, just change into some clean clothes. Annie helped when she saw she was having difficulty getting them on. Larna didn't object. She was way past caring and allowed herself to be dressed like a toddler.

CHAPTER TWENTY-FIVE

The others were waiting in the hall, impatient to be away.

"If it hadn't been for us wasting all this time," said Larna, suddenly feeling guilty, "we might have been able to rescue Yaya and Violet already... "

"I don't believe that, Larna." said Tiblou. "I think they are being used as bait to entrap us. They will be kept alive until they are of no further use. But I feel time is running out now. Whoever is holding Neve and Violet must be running short of patience. So you see the urgency of our situation."

Larna and Aron nodded, their faces serious.

"We must stick together this time," continued Tibs. "We must all watch out for each other during the trek to the Forest of Darkness and hope for a successful outcome."

"Are you going to... whisk yourself there?"

"No, Aron, we walk there. I want to keep an eye on everyone. No more casualties."

"Yeah, okay."

They gathered by the door, which opened and widened enough for them to exit, then returned to its original size. They set off at a brisk march, soon leaving the house with its grey roof and untidy garden behind. As they walked, Larna expected to feel Edsel spying on them from the trees. Nothing. That in itself made her uneasy. But her disquiet was soon replaced by discomfort from her legs. It was one thing to walk around Tiblou's sitting-room in her hinged calipers; it was quite another having to stride through the forest in them. Aron noticed his sister was flagging and tried to cheer her up. "You know, the sooner we rescue Yaya, the sooner we can go home. I mean, back to our *real* home."

Larna's eyes showed a fresh spark of life and she found her

second wind. In spite of their differences, Aron was on her side. She smiled at him. He was a great brother to have and she was proud of him.

* * *

The first thing Larna noticed as they neared the Dark Forest was the silence. All the birds had stopped singing. A tingling sensation ran up her spine and she began to get a nasty feeling about things. She made sure she stuck very close to Aron and the others despite the pain it caused in her legs. Tibs halted in his tracks and looked up. They did the same and saw a trail of red smoke rising into the air above the trees at the centre of the forest.

"We have to follow that smoke," he said. "I have a strong suspicion that's where we will find Neve and Violet."

Automatically closing ranks, they walked into the woods with more caution. The trees were tall, thin, bare and almost black. The closeness of the trees cast even scarier shadows than they were used to. The temperature dropped dramatically and their frosted breath hung in the air like smoke. The light from the sun disappeared to be replaced by a huge dark cloud.

The smoke trail above was getting thicker and redder as they moved closer to their goal. Tibs stopped abruptly and stretched out his arms to prevent them bumping into him. Putting a finger to his lips, he mimed, "Shh!" They stood stock still, quiet as mice, and listened. Larna and Aron were grateful for a few minutes rest, especially Larna whose legs were throbbing mercilessly inside her leg-braces. "I sense Neve and Violet," Tibs whispered. "We're very close. Until I see the next sign, we'll continue on this route."

Apart from the trees, the area was barren. But Tiblou spotted something. As quickly and as quietly as possible, they made their way into a clearing to what looked like a black hole in the ground. But it wasn't. In the middle, a flower stood straight and proud, it's magnificent yellow head bobbing from side to side like a flag blowing in the breeze. Only there wasn't even a draft. The stillness was eerie.

"Goodness has passed this way allowing this one flower to

germinate and grow." Tib's voice was full of emotion. "See how it shines for us."

"What do you mean?" asked Larna.

"I mean Violet and Neve came here – or were brought this way – and left us a trail to follow. I think the bright colour was chosen deliberately to help us." He nodded to himself. "Now for the third sign."

"Does that mean Yaya is close?" Aron asked.

"Yes. I also believe Balgaire's spirit is with us." He closed his eyes for a few seconds. When he opened them they shone with renewed hope. "We need to look for the light and there we'll find our loved ones."

Everyone smiled with relief, but the joy only lasted a moment. A twig snapped nearby.

"They know we are here," said Tibs.

* * *

They formed up in single file and, like school children, put a hand on the shoulder of the one in front. There was no way they were going to be separated again. Plodding on in this fashion, they tried to spot more of the yellow flowers, each one saying a silent prayer to Balgaire for guidance.

Suddenly, Chet broke ranks and began to run. "There's the light. Come on." He raced off to the right. Above the trees and in place of the red smoke there was a white glow that wasn't of their earth. Whilst the rest of them had had their heads down, Chet's had been up. Larna shuddered at the thought that they could have missed this final sign. Each one of them picked up speed. Larna's legs ached like crazy. Bringing up the rear and slowing down with the pain, she was even more determined not to give in.

"Hurry up!" Chet shouted over his shoulder and ran smack-bang into an invisible wall. The others were unable to slow down and hit the wall as well. All of them jumped back and fell over backwards. Tiblou was the first to get up and rub his nose.

"Are you alright, dears?" Annie asked anxiously.

A frustrated Chet replied for them all. "Of course we are! Don't fuss."

Annie looked hurt. She stood up slowly and dusted herself down, trying to hide her face. Tibs put a protective arm round his mother. "Don't take it to heart, mum. This awful place is affecting everybody's mood."

"I'm sorry," Chet added. "Take no notice of me."

Tiblou stepped back a few paces and took what looked like a brand new and slightly bent emerald green wand out of his pocket and pointed it at the invisible wall. "Wish me luck." He raised his arm. ***"REFLECTA EVAPORO!"*** Everyone gasped in surprise as the air in front of them began to shimmer, rippling out like sun on moving water, and the wall disappeared with a loud 'pop'. They took tentative steps forward, hands stretched out in front in case there were other unseen obstacles, but there weren't. They were beginning to celebrate when they were instantly blinded. The brilliance of the light hit them with full force and they automatically put their hands over their eyes until they became accustomed to the glare. Aron was the first to see properly and find his voice.

"YAYA!" he yelled.

Everyone looked up in shock to see Violet and Neve encased in sparkling gold particles all floating around in a huge bubble. Their eyes were closed, as if asleep, with their arms pinned to their sides. It upset Larna to see how restless her grandmother and the fairy were and wondered if they were having a nightmare or were possibly aware of their predicament. Unable to bear this heart-breaking sight, Larna lunged forward and tried to burst the bubble with the tips of her fingers, only to pull them back when a powerful current of electricity shot up her arms. *"ARRGH!"* she screamed and fell backwards into Chet. This was obviously the work of someone very powerful.

Tiblou put the heels of his hands to his temples and closed his eyes. "I can't understand it. I'm sensing a strong dark presence, but don't know where it's coming from." He swayed. "The power from this being is very close to us and trying to take over." The colour drained from the young wizard's face. "I'm having difficulty keeping it at a distance."

"W-W-Who is it?" stammered Aron, trembling from head to toe.

"Well," said a calculating voice, "I'll make it easy for you." They turned to the voice. It came from Chet, but it was Edsel! He had taken over Chet's body in the same way that Balgaire took over Tiblou's when he first appeared, but this was much more sinister and dangerous. In a different body Edsel looked taller, straight backed and he had hair. His skin was ashen but his eyes remained the same. Terrifying!

Larna pushed away from him in disgust, wrinkling her nose at his overpowering smell. It suddenly dawned on her where she'd experienced the foul stench before. Underground! Edsel was one of the stinking Boggrets. Suddenly it all made sense. That night, Edsel must have sent a false message from Neve that made her and her brother wander through the forest on their own. Then he had dispatched her below ground in the hope that she would be disposed of by his foul kin while he pursued Aron above. He wanted rid of both of them, just like Mordrog had done, so the bloodline could not be restored. That meant they were still in terrible danger.

While all this was flashing through Larna's mind, Tiblou was the first to recover from the shock of Edsel's appearance. "Mordrog passed his wand and powers to you, didn't he?"

"No. I took them as he fell." His laugh grated. "Then I pushed him on his way, down the well. He was too busy trying to save himself to take them back." He studied each one of them in turn, eyes glaring from his misshapen head. "Why do you think I put up with him for so many years, at his beck and call and taking punishment for imagined wrongs, eh?" He didn't wait for an answer. "I was studying and learning the whole time. He used me and, in return, I used him. Seems only fair, don't you think?"

Tiblou could see Chet struggling to free himself from Edsel and started playing for time. "Edsel, if we pool our knowledge we can achieve anything... "

"You really don't mean that."

"I do."

"No, you don't." Edsel began to laugh, his top lip curling back to show his contempt.

"If you don't join us you'll just have to suffer the consequences." Tibs warned him.

Cold, calm and utter evil was written on Edsel's face and in his voice. He leaned forward menacingly. "Are you threatening me? Remember whose body I'm using. You wouldn't want to harm your own brother, would you?" He swaggered over to the bubble, appearing to admire his creation and what he'd done to Neve and Violet. Then he turned to Larna and Aron., "It's showdown time, my young friends. I've used the pathetic love you feel for your grandmother to lure you into my clutches. I shall remove you both in an amusing way in due course. Then Mordrog's clever little scheme will come to fruition and I'll have more money I can possibly need for the rest of my days."

"That's not what you're really after though, is it?" said Tiblou.

"You have other plans as well, don't you? A hidden agenda."

"How very perceptive of you, my dear boy! You're quite right. I have taken all of Mordrog's powers. Now I want all of *yours* as well!"

"The only way you will ever get the powers from my son is to kill him and take his wand," said Annie, defiantly.

"And that's exactly what I intend to do," chuckled the Boggret.

"But why?" protested Aron. "Aren't you powerful enough already? Why do you need more?"

"I'll tell you why!" snarled Edsel, suddenly looking furious. "I am a Boggret from the vast land of Tophet below our feet. My father was the ruler there, but his brother Killian murdered him and took his place. My uncle sent his soldiers to hunt me down, but I found a way out and up into this world where I have lived ever since. Now I wish to go home, but not as a fugitive. I shall return as an all-conquering hero. I intend to make my uncle and his family pay for what they've done to my father's household. I will slaughter them all as they did mine. Then I'll be supreme ruler of Sherwood, both above and below ground, and the most powerful warlock of all time!"

CHAPTER TWENTY-SIX

A stunned silence followed this declaration of Edsel's murderous intentions. Larna noticed her grandmother becoming restless, trying to move around inside the bubble of glittery gold. Violet remained perfectly still. The bubble looked as though it was shrinking, losing air, and Larna realised if they didn't free the two of them soon, they would die. Then Neve woke up and began to struggle. Larna willed her to keep still to avoid using up what little oxygen there was left.

For a moment, Edsel remained absorbed in his own thoughts and seemed unaware of Chet trying desperately to regain his body. Then he returned to his senses. Turning to Tiblou, he held out his hand for Balgaire's wand.

"Relinquish the wand without any fuss and your demise will be painless," he promised. "Refuse me and you will die an agonising, lingering death. So will all your kith and kin, including your dear young friends."

"*NO!*" screamed Annie. "Leave my son alone!" For her outburst, she received the full force of one of Edsel's spells and was frozen like a statue. Frantically, Tiblou tried to undo the spell imprisoning his mother, but he failed. He turned on Edsel and brandished Balgaire's wand, ready to retaliate.

"Don't even think about it," growled the warlock. "You're still an infant, taking baby steps. I've been practising in secret for years." He poked his chest. "When you hand over your power to me, I'll free your female protector. Unless she melts first, of course." Edsel grinned.

"You know I can't do that, even if I wanted to. This wand and my cloak were passed on to me strictly in accordance with the rules from the Supreme Council of Wizards and Witches.

Balgaire's power came into me, as he wished, and cannot be transferred."

"Unless you die!" Edsel said.

Then everyone looked up at the ever-shrinking bubble with horrified expressions. The outer skin was starting to cling to Neve, the white witch. It was almost up to her waist. Violet's position was higher up therefore unaffected as yet. Something had to happen soon, otherwise they'd suffocate. Tiblou gave it one last shot, "Why don't you put your new powers to good use and join us? I could learn a lot from you and together we could try to reverse everything Mordrog did to us, and to you."

Edsel's answer was to turn a tree into a spear and send it flying. It pierced the ground in front of Tibs with an almighty thud, the long handle quivering to a stop. Aron yelled frantically and made to charge Edsel. Instantly he was stopped as motionless as Annie. Larna felt a wave of outraged fury at this and, screaming furiously, she went for the monster as well. Another invisible wall stopped her. The electric shock was stronger than the first and it floored her. Lying on the ground groaning, she gave Tibs an imploring look, begging him to do something.

The young wizard rose to the challenge. He waved his wand at the wall, and it disappeared before their captor could counter it. Then Toblou ran hell for leather into Edsel. As they fell, Edsel touched him on the chest with the tip of his wand and sent him sailing backwards. As Tibs hit the ground, feet first, it opened up and began to suck him slowly down, like quicksand. Larna tried to yank him out of the mire but he was stuck firmly. Forgetting her legs, she dropped to her knees and despite the pain tried to doggy-paddle the soil away, only to find she was making it worse. He was going down fast and the more he struggled, the faster he sank. A feeling of helplessness overwhelmed Larna as she saw Aron, Annie, Neve, Violet and now Tibs all powerless to help themselves in the face of Edsel. She sank to the ground, threw back her head and let out a desperate cry for help. Next moment, a puff of wind ruffled her hair and seemed to assault her left cheek and ear. Clamping one hand to the side of her face, she thought she heard a message from the dead. Balgaire! "Larna, look to your inner strength... you have much more than you realise... in your heart and in your hands... you are not so alone as you think... but hurry... hurry... hur... " The voice drifted away on the breeze.

As the bubble lost air, it also lost height and now nearly touched the ground. Edsel's back was towards Larna, unaware that the injured girl could be any threat to him. Nor did he see Clementine, back in the guise of a crow, leaning out of the nearest tree. More importantly, he didn't see the useful little gift she'd dropped down as she flew in. One wing covered her beak as she shook her head, telling Larna to be quiet.

Clementine flew in front of Edsel and sat there making an awful noise, distracting him. Larna picked up the trowel that she'd dropped by her side and began digging the ground in a frenzy. It began to glow, a sulphurous yellow with a bad egg smell, reminding her of the underground tunnels the Boggrets used. Tibs stopped struggling as Larna renewed her efforts and almost had him free. Then Clementine went silent. Edsel was stomping towards Larna, glaring furiously. Her heart was pounding in her chest as she continued to dig frantically, wondering if it was her turn to be turned into something. Instead, he froze her digging arm. Unperturbed, Larna changed hands and shovelled furiously again with the other. Suddenly an unearthly scream filled the air and Edsel stopped dead in his tracks, looked down and yelled again. Clementine had sunk her razor-sharp beak into his fleshy calf and was hanging on for dear life. Thick bloody fluid oozed from the deep gash and ran down his leg. No matter how hard he shook it, she refused to let go.

Larna cringed, hoping Chet couldn't feel the pain, then her arm unfroze and she was able to redouble her efforts until, with a noisy squelchy 'shlurp', Tiblou pulled himself free and shot into the air, regaining his equilibrium and hovering above Edsel's head. Arms crossed, he baited the snarling Boggret, successfully dodging every swing he made.

A quick glance at Neve told Larna that the skin of the bubble clung like a vice and had almost reached her chest.

Edsel managed to shake off the bird and attempted to heal the wound. She had pecked a huge chunk of flesh and spat it out in disgust. The gash was long and deep and wouldn't come together at first. Tibs tried again to free Neve and Violet but he didn't succeed. This gave Edsel time to recoup, become airborne and catch Tiblou on the back with his wand. Hoping to change him into a moth, which would be easy to destroy, he was in too much of a hurry and turned Tibs into a bird of prey by mistake. The young wizard flew out of harm's way, still clutching his wand in one of his talons. Larna was becoming anxious and gave a silent moan. 'Hurry up, Tibs, time's just about to run out!'

At superhuman speed, Tiblou flew back, claws out front, wand transferred to beak and attacked Edsel with great ferocity. Not only did it open up the leg wound again but catapulted the Boggret upwards. He went sailing through the air in a backwards somersault. Yells of pain echoed through the trees as his putrid bloody fluid splashed everything, including onto the bubble. Edsel's blood must have been the nearest thing to pure acid because the outer skin of the bubble began to smoke. So did a few spots on his clothes. Clementine's feathers caught some of it as well. She rolled on the ground to rub it off before it had chance to burn through and reach her flesh.

They came together again. Wizard and warlock tumbled and turned in the air while Larna and Clementine dodged any further acidic fallout. They parted. Tibs flew off. Edsel tried in vain to stem the flow. And Larna wished with all her strength for Tibs to finish it. But what would become of Chet, the 'host' body? Whilst the warlock was preoccupied, the screeching eagle returned at speed and attacked. But in doing so he dropped his wand from his beak and Larna ran to catch it. The second her fingers closed around it, her head was filled with strange words. Over and over until an inner voice told her to repeat them out loud. Pointing the wand at Tiblou and Edsel, she closed her eyes to concentrate, saying in a timid voice, *"EVECTRA ETONA EVICTA."*

"*Will* it! *Mean* it. *LOUDER!*" said the voice in her head.
So she did. Whatever the words meant, she shouted them with such force that her throat tightened and she started to cough. Tiblou immediately returned to his former self and landed safely on the ground.

Edsel took evasive action by hiding behind another protective shield. Tibs had visibly lost strength with his flying antics and wasn't able to resist being pulled towards the shield. It was electrified. As he was drawn through it, sparks flew and the air crackled causing Tibs' body to jerk. He wasn't hurt, just stunned, and Larna gave a huge sigh of relief. Realising she could help again by casting another spell, she waved the warlock's wand and muttered a few words, but they were all wrong. There was a loud bang and she found herself on the other side of the shield. With Tibs... and Edsel! "Help!" she yelled, trying to run back. Edsel stood with a look of surprise on his mean face. He couldn't hide his pain from the bleeding leg and other wounds Clementine and Tibs had inflicted. But as soon as the Boggret started to move, Larna knew she was in serious trouble. Edsel held out his hand for Tiblou's wand and, if murderous looks could kill, Larna thought she was finished.

There was no other choice other than to defend herself and the only means at her disposal was what she was holding. Feeling absolutely terrified she yelled, ***"MONSTRUM HERENDUM TORA!"*** Closing her eyes Larna waited for the worst. There was a terrific whoosh and an explosion. Opening one eye, she was shocked to see Edsel and Tibs on their backs, both out cold. Her eyes opened wide in shock, realising she was responsible for sending them crashing into the shield. Whatever she'd yelled in self-defence had had an effect. Larna rushed to Tiblou's side as fast as her callipered legs would allow and gently prodded him. "Tiblou! Tibs! Are you all right?"

He shook himself and tried to stand. "I think so. Give me a hand." Larna almost overbalanced pulling him up. He grinned and took his wand back from her. "You did well, Larna. I *knew* you could do it!" He felt the side of his head then rubbed the shoulder which had hit the shield first. Then there was movement from Edsel. He was coming round. His moan wasn't the distorted voice of the Boggret – it was Chet's – which reminded them that their situation remained very serious. There was a battle royal going on for possession of Chet's body. He was fighting hard to cast Edsel out for the final time and he seemed to be succeeding.

ut of focus they went. Larna and Tibs watched with a
of fascination and anxiety. Finally, with great effort and
er, Chet forced himself free of the warlock and they
two separate entities again. Chet's face held a look of
ment as he ran his hands down his legs and found no aching
or bloody wounds. Edsel, on the other hand, bore all the
ries and scars Clementine and Tibs had inflicted.

Seeing his brother was alright, Tiblou took advantage of
Edsel's weakened condition. Turning to Aron and Annie, he raised
is wand, touched them and opened his mouth... but nothing
came out. "Calm down, breathe slowly." Chet said. "You're
exhausted." He put his arm around his brother giving moral
support. "Go on, try again." Tibs cocked his left ear, listening. Chet
and Larna looked at each other and nodded. They both knew it
was Balgaire that Tibs was listening to again. *"TEY RAVERTO"*
he chanted, tapping Annie on the shoulder and then repeating it
for Aron. It worked! They began to defrost before their eyes. Tibs
conjured up two soft woollen blankets out of nowhere for the
shivering pair.

Now all eyes turned to the bubble. It was still smoking from
the acid burning through which had relieved the pressure and
allowing some oxygen to enter. But Neve and Violet still needed
rescuing before it was too late. Tiblou hurried towards the tree,
closely followed by Larna and Chet. The shield erected by Edsel
had now dissolved, allowing them free passage. But the evil
creature wasn't finished yet – not by a long chalk. They smelt him
before they saw him. Then he stood before them, barring their
way. Again.

Young wizard and Boggret warlock faced each other for a final
showdown. The hatred radiating from Edsel was like a burning
fire. Heat waves from him forced them to step back a few paces.
He had managed to part-heal his wounds whilst they'd been
preoccupied by the bubble and his leg wasn't bleeding any more.
Absolute dread filled Larna as she realised he wasn't going to give
up. It really was going to be a fight to the end.

But for which one?

CHAPTER TWENTY-SEVEN

Edsel and Tiblou faced each other, squaring up for their make-or-break fight. Larna wished she could do something else to help, but there didn't seem to be anything until Aron started yelling abuse at the Boggret. "Why don't you disappear back to Tophet or wherever stinking place you came from?" he bellowed, making a face and shaking his fist in the air. Annie added her voice to Aron's and that was Larna's cue to join in as well. The three of them shouted threats and insults, making a deafening noise which momentarily distracted the warlock and allowed Tibs to get the first punch in via a spell. Edsel flew backwards into a tree. Tiblou didn't waste any time and followed up his attack whilst he had the advantage. His second spell bounced off the Boggret, sending out showers of deadly sparks which broke into miniature fires. But it had the effect of making Edsel lose his wand. It went sailing through the air and bounced off the bubble on its way down, causing the bubble to zip open and drop Neve and Violet in a heap on the ground. Looking very much worse for wear from their ordeal, they began to retch and cough. The gold fluid from inside the bubble drained out, drenching them. They spat it out. Within seconds it was on the move, gradually sliding off them and forming puddles at their feet. Then it simply faded away. They were bone dry, their clothes having miraculously dried as it dropped off them. Soon, there was no evidence of the liquid gold ever existing.

This diversion worked to Edsel's advantage. With everyone's eyes focused on the release of Neve and Violet from their deadly prison, he issued a whooshing fireball from his fingertips that nobody was expecting. It would have taken Tibs' head off had it not been for the urgent warning given by Clementine. She cawed loudly, causing the young wizard to duck at the last moment. The fireball seared over his head and disappeared into the dark forest like a comet in the night sky. Edsel stamped his foot in fury and that was enough to hand the initiative back to Tibs. The young wizard cast a third spell that engulfed the warlock in a shimmering light and then imprisoned him in a cage suspended from a tree. Bound and gagged, he was unable to move or cast spells. Everyone cheered with relief. They were safe at last.

Violet unfurled, slowly and gracefully. In a musical voice she asked, "What has happened?" Annie explained as briefly as possible that she and Neve had been kidnapped by Edsel and held prisoner. Neve started patting herself down and looking anxious. "Where's my wand? I had it with me in the bubble."

"It must have fallen out when you were released," said Tibs. "We must find it before anything else happens." He raised his own wand and mumbled a few words. "Now stand back and perfectly still." Soon the ground began to move beneath them. And there was Neve's wand, trying to poke its head out of the earth like a growing flower in a speeded-up nature film. As Neve bent to pick it up, it pulled itself free, shook off the damp soil and floated up to her outstretched hand.

"One down, one to go," commented Chet.

"What do you mean?" From Aron.

"Edsel's wand. The one that flew through the air and punctured the bubble. We've got to find it and make sure he doesn't get his hands on it again."

Without another word, everyone scattered in different directions and began to search. Larna's legs were hurting and she could see grazes where the metal callipers had rubbed. A trickle of blood had run down both legs and dried. The woods were creepy. Intimidating. And it didn't help that Edsel's struggles in the cage were furious and noisy.

Larna was so engrossed in the search, she didn't see her brother move to investigate a clump of trees. Head down, searching through piles of rotting vegetation, Aron didn't see or feel anything until it was too late. They only knew he was in trouble when he cried out in terror, *"HELP!"* Everyone ran towards him, Larna limping as best she could. They came to an abrupt halt. He'd been rummaging around in the tree roots and tried to pull one out of the ground, mistakenly thinking it was the wand. Unfortunately, he'd woken something from its dormant state and it had wrapped its fingers round his ankles. Each time any one of them went close enough to help, other tree hands came out of the earth and waved about, trying to grab them.

They could only watch in dismay as the branches travelled up and around Aron's body, trying to draw him into the trunk.

"What's happening, Yaya?" gasped Larna.

"He's disturbed the Dryads and they've taken him. If he touches the bark of the tree, he'll be turned to stone.

Feeling she must do something, Larna picked up a stone and threw it at the tree with all her might. It was a mistake. The surrounding trees woke up and gnarled hands clawed their way up through the soil to find them. No matter how hard any of them struggled, there was no way to escape their clutches. And all the time Aron moved closer and closer to the trunk.

Tiblou tried using his magic powers, but to no avail. They were firmly stuck and beginning to panic. Each time Neve cast a spell, it also bounced off, as if the tree was batting it away. Then she suddenly remembered her grandmother telling her that the Dryads thrived only on fear, "This may sound crazy, but don't struggle. Relax! Let the trees pull us towards them and... "

Chet butted in, "We'll be crushed."

"Just *do* it. And when you touch the tree, embrace it. Give it some love. Think happy thoughts. On no account think of fear or hatred!"

It seemed strange advice, but it was worth a try. The situation was desperate. Shutting her eyes tightly, Larna wrapped her arms around the rough trunk and put her heart and soul into thoughts of happier times, projecting them at the tree. The others did the same. Aron muttered something about feeling a daft idiot hugging an inanimate object. Then silence. Larna lost herself in wonderful dreams of home and thoughts of her mum and how she made their world brighter and happier. She missed her.

Larna had no idea how long she stood there, hugging the tree for dear life. But a gradual sensation of well-being drifting into her mind that made her aware of where she was and what she was doing. She wasn't being squeezed to death, just held there gently, the lower branches holding her up. The others were experiencing something similar as they stepped back. Larna's injured legs felt numb, so she slid down onto the ground, looked up and said a tearful, "Thank you," to her captor. Then she watched as the hands became roots again and shrank back and disappeared under the soil. She gazed in wonder at their transformation as the dark trees began to show signs of life. Chet pulled Larna up and helped her over to the others. Annie made an attempt to mother them all, then gave up, and sat transfixed at the wonderful sight unfolding in front of them. New growth appeared on the branches. Buds were popping and slowly becoming healthy green leaves.

"Now what's happening?" Aron wanted to know.

"Love," answered Neve, triumphantly. "We've been saved by the power of love."

"Were you certain, Yaya?" queried Larna. "Did you positively and absolutely know it would work?"

Looking down her nose, and with a playful glint in her eyes, Yaya said, "That's for me to know and for you to find out!"

Annie brought them back to reality. "We're supposed to be looking for a Edsel's missing wand, remember?"

Everyone fanned out again and resumed the search for Edsel's deadly wand. They trudged through the gloomy forest, looking everywhere, and were about to give up when Larna saw something move out of the corner of her eye. Nudging Aron excitedly, she pointed upwards.

"Well, of all the places !" Aron exclaimed.

Larna shouted to the others, "I've found it. Look up in the trees. Edsel's wand."

It was lodged in the highest branch of the tallest trees. Like a hunted animal, it sensed it had been found and inched its way along the branch ready to fly off again. But Tibs was too quick for it. He shot into the air and grabbed it firmly in one hand. Then he floated down and handed it to Neve in the hope she'd know what to do with it. With a bit of jiggery-pokery she managed to tuck it into her pocket without it sticking out. Then everyone broke into cheers.

It was a happy band that made its way back to the clearing where Edsel was imprisoned. Laughing and joking, patting each other on the back, they relished the feeling that their troubles were finally over. Mordrog was no more. Edsel was a prisoner and his powerful wand was in their possession. Their enemies were defeated. They had won!

Discussing how best to celebrate their victory, everyone marched into the clearing. Larna was the first to notice it was strangely quiet. She glanced up and felt the blood drain from her face. "L-L-Look!" she stammered. The others followed her gaze and they too went white with horror. The tree prison lay in tatters with Clementine fluttering on the ground beside it, mortally injured. And Edsel was gone!

* * *

The shocked silence that followed only lasted a few seconds. It was broken by a blinding flash and everyone found themselves frozen like statues in a park. They couldn't move or speak. They were completely helpless. Then a familiar disgusting smell reached their noses and the Boggret stepped out from behind one of the trees. His face was black with fury and it was clear he was intent on revenge of the cruellest kind.

"I expect you're wondering how I managed to do that given I don't have my wand," he cackled in his hateful high-pitched voice. "Well, I'll tell you. I have three reserve spells in my fingertips at all times. I keep them there for emergencies and they renew themselves an hour-or-so after they've been used. I've just deployed one... and the other two are reserved for your deaths. Your *painful* deaths."

He strode round his prisoners with a gleeful sneer on his face, turning first to Larna and Aron. "I said I'd dispose of you in an amusing fashion," he chuckled, "and so I shall. I'm a Boggret of my word." Fire sizzled from the ends of his fingers and the ground around the terrified brother and sister began to burn. The flames began creeping towards them. Soon they would go up in smoke. Then the warlock turned his attention to the others. "One of you has my wand," he sneered, "but I can't be bothered to search you all. I'm very busy. So I shall simply make you all disappear, leaving the wand behind when you are no more." This time a bolt of blue light shot out from his fingers and buzzed round the remaining line of prisoners like electricity. Everyone's feet began to fade in and out of view, then their lower legs. The spell would soon work its way up their bodies and dissolve them away to nothing.

Edsel sat down on a tree-stump to watch the slow demise of his enemies. But he had forgotten what time it was. A sudden thunderclap overhead signalled the arrival of the daily downpour. The rain lashed down onto the flames surrounding Larna and Aron, putting them out with a sizzle. And the water also reversed the other spell so that everyone's legs became visible again and their faces unfroze enough to register a hint of relief from the pain.

Cursing furiously because he had no more spells at his disposal, the Boggret warlock strode over to Tiblou and snatched his wand out of his hand.

"This'll do instead!" he chuckled. "I'll dispose of you all with one of your own spells and take possession of *both* the wands. Then I will have won this tiresome battle."

Larna, Aron and their friends waited for the end as Edsel waved Tibs' wand in the air and chanted some strange words. Then something amazing happened. Instead of the flames rekindling round Larna and Aron's legs, they found themselves freed! The two of them were still trying to rub some movement back into their stiff limbs when Edsel tried another spell. This time, their grandmother and all the others were released. They lumbered towards their enemy as fast as their stiff bodies would allow and, in desperation, he launched a third and final spell at them, The result of this one was astounding. Edsel shrank down into a large black rat with a long tail and evil red eyes. Squeaking shrilly, he scurried off into the shadowy undergrowth.

In the stunned silence that followed, Aron was the first to find his voice. "What happened there?"

"A miracle," replied Tiblou, picking up his wand from the ground. "This beautiful thing is incapable of casting an evil spell. It can only work for good. Edsel made a big mistake when he thought he could use it for his cruel purposes."

* * *

It was Violet who remembered Clementine's plight. She flew over to the small mound of black feathers on the path ahead of them, waving furiously. The bird was still alive – but only just.

"Is there anything you can do?" Larna asked her grandmother.

"I'm not sure, love," she replied. "Tiblou?"

He shook his head. "I don't know." He raised his head. "I need help."

Almost immediately a jumbled pattern formed overhead, then a sunbeam shone transforming it into a hologram of Balgaire. He kept fading to almost nothing then back again, as if an intermittent surge of power strengthened him.

"I haven'... much time, so list... carefully. Just... yond the Forest of Darkness... ere are three trees which you wi... recognise as... oon as you see th.m... " The air crackled and the picture broke up.

"Then what?" Larna asked the air.

Balgaire reappeared and continued, "Place Clemen... in the mid... and circle... em. Tiblou and Neve must chant the Enduesa... "

"But, I thought that spell was a myth." Tiblou said.

"No. It's existence h... to be protected from... e likes... Mordrog... Eds... "

Tiblou was beginning to panic. "I don't know it, Balgaire."

Another surge of power. "Repeat... , *CLEMENTINE VITA REVERTO TORA.*"

He did.

"Do *NOT* f... get. What happens afterwards will take care of... self th... s no guarantee " He was breaking up and fading rapidly. "best hope for Clem... tine. Last time... here. Farewell friends ... "

With that he was gone.

The very nature of the situation put them on automatic pilot. Tiblou held Clementine to his chest and started running towards the edge of the forest and the light. Chet bundled Larna onto his back like a sack of potatoes and as best he could hurried after him. The others followed suit. Balgaire had been correct. They did recognise the three trees as soon as they saw them. They were half the size of any of the others and the most startling shade of plum they'd ever seen. They were swaying in a warm gentle breeze and looked breath-taking.

Neve held out her arms saying urgently, "Give her to me." She ran to the middle of the trees and placed the small body on the ground in the middle of a dip. She tapped Clementine's head with her right hand finger tips and her chest with the left. She bent her head for a fraction of a second then re-joining the others. Slightly out of breath she ordered, "Quickly, circle the trees." They took it for granted that she knew what she was doing and did as bid. Tiblou tried to remember the spell, but in his haste he must have got it wrong. Nothing happened. Neve prompted, and then repeated it with him. Nothing. In sheer frustration, Larna silently said the spell with her and Tibs, *"CLEMENTINE VITA REVERTO TORA!"*

The soil under the crow changed colour, went darker. Seconds later the dip filled with royal blue water completely submerging the little body. Everyone held their breath as the rays of the setting sun played on the gently moving fluid like thousands of tiny diamonds. They had just about given up hope when a spout of water shot up from the middle of the pool. They burst into nervous laughter when a very cross bird was balanced on top, making noises like squawking coughs and struggling to get off.

"Well, isn't anybody going to help me?" Clementine complained as the water spout lowered their friend. At the same time the pool evaporated, leaving her in the middle of a dry dip. She examined her feathers and claws. "You all took your time!"

CHAPTER TWENTY-EIGHT

Chet was the first to react to Clementine's miraculous recovery. "You gave us one heck of a scare, Clementine. We thought the worst."

"So did I, my boy!"

"What happened to you?" asked Annie.

"Edsel," answered the bird. "I made the mistake of perching in his tree and he hypnotised me. I had no choice but to obey his will and peck away his prison and his bindings."

"So *that's* how he escaped!" said Larna.

"When he was free, he threw me to the ground like an old rag. Talk about ungrateful!"

"Boggrets are never grateful for anything kind," commented Tibs.

"Where is the ghastly creature now?" asked Clementine, shakily standing upright and returned to human form, visibly regaining her strength.

"He's where he belongs and won't harm us – or anybody else – ever again."

"Famous last words," commented Clementine, waggling a long slender finger.

To prove her point, Neve produced Edsel's evil black wand and showed it to her friend.

"You'd better get rid of that," she advised. Then added, "And never say never!"

With that, Clementine turned and sauntered off, heading to the portal she guarded with her twin. Just before she vanished into the trees, she swivelled her head and a faint "Thank you" was heard wafting on the breeze.

"Right, then," said Neve. "My job here is done. Time to head back to Tiblou's and finish what you started, don't you think? Unless after all you've been through you two have changed your minds?"

"Of course not," answered Aron, sidling up to Larna. "I gave my word. We both did."

Laughing with relief and expectation, everyone made their way back to Tiblou's new home. The return journey from the Forest of Darkness was much slower than the outward one. Aron was flagging with tiredness and Larna's sore legs meant she needed to be helped again. But eventually they reached the quirky house and Tibs ordered the front door to open to allow everyone into the entrance hall.

To the right of the front door stood a tall, slim pine bookcase stacked with books of all shapes and sizes. The covers were mostly red and neatly filed in alphabetical order by author. Looking up, the ceiling resembled a summer sky in the early evening. It looked so realistic that for a second Larna was fooled into thinking she was still outside. There were three windows, one on the right and two on the left which looked out onto the gardens. Two internal doors, apart from the front entrance, became visible. One was at the far end of the room and the other to Larna's right, almost hidden by the end of the bookcase.

They all jumped when the huge grandfather clock struck. It reminded Larna and Aron of their grandmother's cottage and they both felt a yearning to be back there. "Surely it's not that time already. I'd quite lost track." Annie said.

"And we haven't even had a drink yet." moaned Aron.

Tiblou shot forward and told them to follow. "I'm afraid you can't afford to relax yet. We're running out of time. Some of my friends have changed almost to the point of no return, so it might be too late for them." He went to the fireplace, stepped onto the hearth and prepared to walk into the flames. Horrified, Larna grabbed the wizard's sleeve and pulled him back. "Tibs, what on earth are you doing?"

He shook Larna off. "Have a little faith," he sighed, tapping his temple. "Haven't you learned anything since you've been here? You know, mind over matter and all that! " He took Larna's arm and dragged her toward the flames. To her astonishment, the flames parted like the Dead Sea for Moses, allowing them to pass through. The others followed, walking in single file, before the flames joined up again. They faced a bright orange door which creaked as it began to open. Then they all crowded together until a light came on and they found they were able to spread out, allowing Tiblou some breathing space. Neve was the last one in and remained with her back to the door, watching.

At the far end stood two armchairs, a side table and a bookshelf against the wall to the left. The rest of the room was bare. It seemed familiar and felt strangely comforting.

"Aren't those Balgaire's chairs?" Aron asked.
Tiblou took their elbows and guided them towards the chairs. "No more questions. It's time. Sit down please and leave the rest to me. Okay?"

Larna and Aron looked sideways at each other, lost in the deep cushions. Aron made a funny face in an attempt to make his sister laugh, but she didn't. This was serious stuff, not a laughing matter, and he quickly sobered up.

"Remember the drill? Elbows resting on chair arms?" Tibs reminded them.

They nodded, swallowing hard. Now it had finally come to it, they both felt a bit nervous. But they had given their word and the burning desire to help their friends overrode their fear.

Tibs looked at his mother. "Do you know where the serum is?"

Annie nodded and marched to the bookcase. On tiptoe, and after a couple of attempts, she managed to pull out a tome which balanced precariously on the edge of the shelf. It was large and heavy and her knees gave a fraction as it fell off the shelf into her arms. Larna attempted to go and help but was unable to leave the chair. Annie staggered over to Tibs who took the huge book from her as if it were as light as a feather and placed it on the floor between their chairs. Larna and Aron looked down and recognised it from before at Balgaire's. Tibs tapped the hard front cover with his wand and muttered a few unintelligible words. The book opened up to reveal the two crystal vials still securely held in place by a tiny pair of hands with long red curved finger nails. As Tiblou bent to remove the vials, the hands released their grip and crossed themselves on top of a cloud of silky substance. Slowly the book closed and returned to its rightful place on the shelf unaided. Nobody would ever guess that it had been moved.

Tibs magically stood the vials on the side table. They began to wobble, causing everyone to gasp. With one look from Tiblou, the vials immediately stopped in an upright position. An audible sigh of relief echoed round the room. Then he produced an unusual pen-like object from under the table top. Holding it up in his right hand, he approached Larna and Aron.

"This is it." Tibs said. "What you've been brought here for. Are you ready?"

They both leaned over the side of their chairs, touching shoulders, and turned to their grandmother. Still with her back against the door, she gave them a reassuring smile and nod of consent. That was all the encouragement they needed and they exclaimed in unison, *"YES!"* Removing their jackets, they rolled their sleeves as far as they would. "Relax." said Tibs. "Close your eyes and count to three."

With her eyes tightly shut, Larna listened to Tibs' voice. It had a hypnotic effect and she felt herself sinking into the chair. It felt sssoo comfortable, she didn't want to move. They both began to count, their words sounding slurred and distant as if they were falling asleep. "Onnne ... Twooo ... Threee... "

"Open your eyes, it's all over. Well done!"

Instantly wide awake, Larna turned to see if her brother was okay. He was giving her the once-over as well. Studying each other's arms, still resting on the chair, Larna found the faintest red suction ring with a little dot right in the middle.

Grinning, Aron said, "I never felt a thing. I'm impressed."

"And I'm relieved it's over," added Larna. "It *is* all over, isn't it?"

CHAPTER TWENTY NINE

With his left hand Tiblou picked up the nearest vial and gently blew on it. The lid immediately began to unfurl. With his right he attached the business-end of the pen to it, slowly depressing the top and sending some of the blood cascading into the crystal. Then he repeated the whole process into the second one before shaking both gently from side to side. Everyone watched, mesmerised, as Larna and Aron's blood mixed with the serum. It began very slowly, circling, and then separating again. Suddenly, strands of the donated blood broke away and began to dart around, seemingly targeting something live inside the tubes before absorbing it and looking for the next. It was like a miniature fireworks display in each vial.

Larna broke the suspense by asking, "What happens now?"

Tiblou held up the two crystal vials letting the light catch the contents. They shone, but when he ordered the room lights off, they emitted an incandescent glow. Satisfied the process was working, he ordered the lights on again. "I will use one of these for our own purposes and hand the other over for duplication."

"What'll happen if you run out?" Aron asked concerned.

"We won't let that happen," said Annie, pulling Aron out of the chair and put her arms round him. He squirmed with embarrassment. "Oh no, dear. We have been preparing for this for over a century. Some of the antidote will be stored, just in case... " she patted the top of his head. Aron pulled one of his funny pained faces. "We've waited a long time for you two, haven't we, Neve?"

Larna and Aron looked at their grandmother, shocked. She must have known about this all the time and never let on. Making them promise not to wander too far into the forest was a clever piece of psychology on her part, knowing it would only make them want to do it all the more. And the repeated advice to stick together at all times made sense now, too. Yaya had known exactly what she was doing and, with a great deal of luck and her secret role as The White Witch of Sherwood, it had paid off.

"It's time," was all Tiblou said and made for the exit. They followed in single file, back through the fire, into the sitting room and out of the front door into the garden.

"Time?" Aron whispered. "To go home?"

"Not quite yet," Neve answered. "Have patience. Won't be long now."

Outside, Neve instructed everyone to form a protective circle round Tiblou. With a new lease of life, Violet flew onto the scene and perched herself on his shoulder. Larna placed herself to the wizard's left and Aron to the right, peeping at each other out of the corner of their eyes and waiting with bated breath. Tibs drew his wand out of one of the pockets of his robe and pointed it upwards to the sky. "As this spell directly concerns you both," he explained, looking at them each in turn, "it is in your tongue. You need to focus on the words and will them into being if it's to work properly." Then everyone bowed their heads as he chanted,

"Bring the sky alight
And with all my might
Bring forth much joy
To all in sight."

He paused for breath and to think how to continue. Then he thrust the wand as high as he could, the other arm stretched upwards too.

"With this gift so freely given
Lift this curse so we be shriven.
And as this serum now is pure,
Let everyone enjoy the cure!"

A magnificent bolt of light shot from the wand and spread out above them, leaving a star in its wake. It hovered high in the sky, directly above Tiblou, a beacon letting everyone know Tibs had the antidote and it was time to gather for their first taste of the miracle cure. Annie noticed that Tiblou had grown in stature and had lost most of his boyishness. He had grown up. She felt a pang of regret for the loss of her child, but proud that he was doing what he was always meant to do in order to walk in Balgaire's shoes and fulfil his destiny. She had no doubt that in time Tiblou the man would be a terrific wizard. One of the best.

The ground began to shake and birds fluttered from the trees. An air of expectancy hovered all around them. There was movement and noise in the forest. The first to emerge was Uncle Roger, bringing with him a steady stream of customers from his café. It had begun! They were the first wave of part mutants all desperately sharing the same dream – to be complete humans again before it was too late and they changed beyond the point of no return. More and more came out of the forest, all shapes and sizes.

The plight of one particular family touched Larna more than any of the others. Each one of them was neither one animal nor another, but a hotchpotch of several. The mother had patchy black and white fur from various long and short-haired cats. The father had large donkey ears and the big brown eyes of a cow. And the children were a mixture of dog and bird. They all looked comical and repulsive at the same time and Larna longed for them to be cured.

She stood beside them with Aron and listened to Tiblou's speech to the assembled crowd, explaining why everyone had been summonsed.

"Thanks to Larna and Aron's incredible gift," he said, "we now have the means to reverse the disease inflicted on us generations ago." He looked around at the still gathering crowd. "It may not be 100% successful for some of us, but it should halt further mutation. Can I have a show of hands of those who want the antidote?"

There was an immediate sea of hands and paws and other means of acceptance.

"Anyone wish to opt out?"

Not one person. There was an eerie silence which sent shivers of excitement down Larna's spine. Aron felt it too.

"Finally, we need to point out that we haven't had time to test this new serum, so the first person must be a volunteer."

The silence deepened. Each person looked to their neighbour to see who would be brave enough to step forward. Some stepped back a few paces amid mutterings. Then Uncle Roger strode out of the crowd and stood in front of Tiblou.

"I have lived my life like this so far," patting his chest with clenched fists, "and I fancy a change for the rest of it." He half turned to the crowd and added loudly, "I'll be your first volunteer. Go ahead, nephew."

He held out his arm, but Tibs shook his head. "It doesn't work that way, Uncle." Then he drew his wand over the crystal vial and tapped it gently.

"Hear ye, hear ye," he chanted,

"Change all back to what they should be!"

Lifting his thumb from the flat end of the vial, it opened up allowing a little of the fluid to slowly wind out. Everyone stared in wonder as the fluid doubled, then multiplied itself hundreds of times. The sky was full of spiralling multi-coloured DNA strands. A drop separated from the rest and hovered over Uncle Roger like a brilliant pink raindrop.

"Take it, it's yours." Tibs told him.

With a final nervous glance at his family, Uncle Roger opened his mouth to catch the drop, and swallowed. Within seconds he fell to his knees, looking upwards to the heavens and the glittering stars. His eyes rolled back. The crowd backed away, making noises of fear and disappointment. Larna and Aron stayed put beside the hotchpotch family and watched in awe as Uncle Roger's canine ears, nose and the other features slowly disappeared and his eyes returned to normal. He looked up at Tibs, gave a little shake, and calmly asked...

"Well? Has it worked?"

"See for yourself, Uncle."

An enormous mirror materialised out of nowhere. Still on his knees, Uncle Roger saw himself as if for the first time, slowly running his hands over his face, his head and his ears. He kept repeating, "Oh! Oh!" Then, "I look... like our guests... Normal!" He was fighting back tears of emotion. Standing, he ran his hands over the front of his body, then behind. He stopped suddenly when his tail wagged.

Larna heard a quiet, "uh-oh!" from her brother.

"We've failed you," moaned Tibs.

Pulling himself up to his full height, Uncle Roger laid his hands on the young wizard's shoulders. "Don't be silly, young man, I'm thrilled." He looked round at his tail. "I am disappointed to be left with this ... but I can't thank you enough for the rest of me." Pausing for a second he added, "I'll look upon it as a reminder of who I truly am... or rather was. Now, does that put your mind at ease?" He turned and faced the crowd, spread his arms and shouted, "Well, I'm still here. What are you waiting for?"

A tremendous noise erupted, heralding a sudden stampede for the serum. Tibs held up his arms. *NO!* he yelled. "Please stand still." He looked at the multitude. "Look to the sky and open your mouth. That's all you have to do."

The crowd hesitated.

Then the hotchpotch parents lifted the chin of each of their children and gently pressed the sides of their mouth until they opened to receive a drop of the precious antidote. The adults followed suit. And the transformations began. From the ugliest children Larna and Aron had ever seen came twin boys and a beautiful baby girl. All three were perfect. So were their mother and father once their changes were complete. They turned to face the crowd and there was a massive intake of breath. Then all faces tilted skywards, mouths opened, catching and swallowing a droplet of the serum. Almost immediately they too began to experience changes of varying degrees. Some completely, others not fully. Nevertheless, everyone seemed to be happy.

Chet leaned towards Tibs and said in a low voice, "Well now, Mr Miracle-Worker, seeing as mum and I decided to wait until last in case there wasn't enough for everybody, don't you think you'd better give us some of that stuff before it loses its potency?"

Tibs looked mortified. "Yes, yes, yes!" He shook the container vigorously, repeated the rhyme and released the last of the serum. The spirals of DNA flew up and hovered over Annie and Chet before dropping into their open mouths. The changes were immediate and Annie hugged both sons, tears streaming down her face. Then they noticed, like Roger, that they too had failed to get rid of their tails. They looked at each other, shrugged their shoulders and burst out laughing. Larna, Aron and Tibs couldn't help but join in. It released the tension and, afterwards, everyone felt much better for it.

CHAPTER THIRTY

All this time Neve and Violet had remained in the background keeping an eye on the throng witnessing the exhilaration and raw emotion as people changed. Jubilant shouts of everything. With great satisfaction, they'd observed Tiblou's skill as a wizard and thanks to Tiblou, Aron and Larna echoed in their ears as the crowd gradually began to disperse

Neve started to move towards her grandchildren. Putting her arms around their shoulders, she asked if there was anything they would like to do before going home. Suddenly Larna felt herself engulfed by an overwhelming sadness as she realised they were about to leave these wonderful people. Aron was not so sensitive. A huge smile split his face, almost ear to ear. "Are you kidding? There's only one place I want to visit. Roger's Kitchen Café!"

Larna was surprised and more than a little humbled at how many people had stayed behind to thank them personally, or pat their backs as they made their way through the woods to the cafe. Most of them left it at that, but others followed adding to the crowd waiting for them inside the cheerful room. Two tall glass dessert dishes filled with miniature balls of rainbow ice cream were ceremoniously placed in front of Larna and Aron. Puffs of strawberry-scented vapour escaped from the top and wafted under their noses, making them both drool. Then they noticed there were no spoons beside the glasses. How were they meant to eat this delicious-looking treat? They were about to ask Uncle Roger for some cutlery when the ice-cream seemed to come alive. It started fizzing about in the glasses and then, with a bang, a multi-coloured ice cream ball from each one shot into the air and hovered above Larna and Aron, waiting for them to open their mouths. When they did, it dropped onto their tongues, filling their senses with the most exquisite flavours. Immediately, they opened their mouth for more and two more balls shot up from the glasses... and continued doing so until they were completely full.

"Astounding!" exclaimed Larna, licking her lips. "Exploding ice cream!"

"Can I have a doggie bag to take some home with me, please?" asked Aron.

"Sorry, my friend," replied Uncle Roger. "That's an impossibility. I understand food doesn't travel, backwards or forwards through time!"

When the treat was over, Neve appeared at her grandchildren's side. "Right, you two," she said in her usual no-nonsense manner. "It really is time to return now."

"Can't we stay the night and go home in the morning?" wheedled Aron.

"No, we have to avoid being spotted by the tourists visiting Sherwood Forest. Think of the trouble it would cause if we suddenly appeared, from nowhere, as if by magic."

"These are Tiblou's clothes," said Larna. "Please could we just make a detour via his place? I've got to change."

Neve glanced at her watch. "As you wish. We won't go the normal way though. Say goodbye to everyone."

Those who didn't shake their hands muttered their grateful thanks. Then, flanked by his customers, Uncle Roger followed them outside. "It's a shame you can't take anything back, but I would like you to know that your dessert will now be known as The Gorry Surprise from now on."

Before they had a chance to thank him, the two of them were unceremoniously yanked through space and arrived at Tiblou's house with Neve, Annie, Tibs and Chet.

"Whoa!" Aron steadied himself on a chair back. "What just happened? That was fantastic!"

Neve clapped her hands, "Come on, please. Upstairs to collect your gear. Larna, go and get changed and meet me back here as quickly as you can. "

Twisting the acorn on top of the newel posts, Larna and Aron sailed upstairs on the step and made their way to the bedroom to fetch their things. But Larna couldn't find hers. Suddenly she remembered that Annie had bundled her scruffy torn dressing gown and pyjamas down the chute.

"OH, NO!" she exclaimed.

"What's the problem?"

"When I was brought back from the underworld, the dressing gown and pyjamas Tiblou leant me were ripped to ribbons, so Annie disposed of them."

"So? What's the big deal? We're returning home in our own clothes."

"The clothes aren't what upsets me. It's a present Cai gave me on behalf of his father, King Drisco, just before they left me to find a safe passage back underground. It was in the dressing gown pocket. He made me promise not to lose it. And I have! Larna was surprised by how much it upset her. "What'll I do, Aron?"

Her brother frowned. "Hang on a minute, he won't know. There's no way he'll find out, is there? And besides, you won't be going down there again, so you two won't ever meet, will you?"

The thought of never seeing Cai again hit her with a thump in her chest. To hide any confusion, she sat on the bed and tried to scratch her legs where the metal calliper was rubbing again. She leant too far forwards and tumbled off. Her yells of pain brought the others racing upstairs.

"What's happened now?"

"It's alright, Yaya, I slipped off the bed and hurt myself. It's not so bad now. Honestly."

Neve knelt in front of Larna and inspected the metal frames. "We will have to do something about these when we get home. No time now." She put both hands on the edge of the bed to push herself up. "Just a minute, your knee is bleeding. You've cut it on something sharp." She ran her hand over the wooden floor and found something sticking up between the floor boards. She pulled and waggled it as hard as she could, but it refused to come out.

"Let me try, Yaya," said Larna. Without any force, the object came out in her hand like King Arthur's sword out of the stone. They all gasped. "It's my present from Cai and his father!"

"What is it?" asked Aron, curiously.

"I have absolutely no idea, but whatever it is, I won't lose it again." Gingerly running her fingers all over the gold disc, she couldn't find anything sharp on it. It was as if it was asking to be found.

In a tremulous voice Annie said, "It is, or it was, a gift from me to my husband, Zebedia." She held out her hand and, without a word, Larna placed the disc in it. Looking shocked and emotional, the old lady turned to address Tibs and Chet. "I gave this to your father on the day he disappeared." She pressed a hidden spring and the disc slowly opened, like flower petals unfurling. A beam of light shone upwards and to everyone's surprise except Annie's, they saw moving pictures of children playing and laughing in a garden somewhere. The sound effects were a bit tinny at first until the picture fanned out to three times the size of the disc and grew to approximately a foot in height.

Tears trickled down Annie's face. Chet and Tiblou just stood and watched, pale and shocked. The others were a captive audience.

"My boys. When they were very small." She paused, a tiny smile raised the corner of her lips. "They tormented the life out of me to make this... "

"So our father would always have us with him. I remember, mum." Chet put a comforting arm round his mother's shoulders.

Tibs was fascinated and bent towards the picture. "I think I remember it as well. I was about two or three, wasn't I?"

A very young Annie entered the frame and encouraged the children to wave.

"Love you, Papa Zeb," The children broke into fits of giggles having dared to call their father Zeb. Next moment the light shrivelled back into the disc and the petals closed.

For a few seconds there was complete silence. Then Annie, Chet and Tiblou began asking questions all at the same time. Neve held up a hand. "One at a time, please, or we will be here all night. Now, Larna, can you remember anything else about this disc? This is very important."

"I know. I'm already racking my brains trying... Cai said King Drisco found it in one of the caves. No, that's not strictly true."

She scratched her head. "Just a minute ... he found it in one of the passages leading out of a cave."

Chet shook his head in disbelief. "But, how did it get there? We've grown up believing Dad went to join the search party for Aunty June when she disappeared. She was never found either."

"I know everybody thought the worst. It was years after they went missing that Roger discovered that my sister may possibly be still alive down there somewhere in the underworld." Annie sighed. "But nobody, not even Balgaire, could find out anything about my husband's disappearance."

Silence again. Violet whispered in the witch's ear, then raising an eyebrow Neve said quietly. "There might be a way." Everybody leaned slightly forward, silently urging her to continue, "Follow the disc!"

"What do you mean?" Larna wanted to know.

"Use its memory," Neve said.

"I don't understand," murmured Aron.

"Zebedia obviously suffered an extremely traumatic experience whilst this photo-disc was in his possession. So let me, Tiblou and Violet see if we can follow its memory-trail. If it has one, that is." Neve must have thought Annie needed more persuasion. "For instance, old houses supposedly absorb joyful events as well as sad ones. So, maybe it applies to other things as well – like this. Anyway, it's worth a try. What do you think?"

Annie's sad look turned to anticipation. She sucked in her bottom lip. "Oh, yes please. If it works it will bring an end to the awful nightmare of not knowing what happened to my dear husband."

Neve, Tibs and Violet formed a triangle, each holding the edge of the disc with their right hand. In Violet's case, she had some difficulty because of her size but, as determined as ever, she coped. The white witch told them to stand perfectly still and be quiet whilst they concentrated. Annie, Chet, Aron and Larna all looked on with bated breath.

CHAPTER THIRTY-ONE

The three holding the disc froze. The rest of them took a massive intake of breath and held it. Even the birds outside the bedroom window seemed to think something momentous might be about to happen and were silent.

After a few more minutes of nothing happening, Larna's concentration began to waver. Her legs were ready to give up on her and she was about to fall over when, inside the triangle, a haze appeared. Like smoke, it billowed upwards and began to take shape. Another silent film showed Zebedia accepting the disc and putting it in his top pocket. It wasn't deep enough, so about a third of the photo-disc remained visible. He bent, patted the children on the head and then gave Annie a big hug. She handed him what looked like a packed lunch. They exchanged a few words then he turned and walked into the woods, joining some others who were waiting for him.

Deep in the forest, very close to the Dark Side, they must have decided to separate because Zebedia was alone from then on. They could see but not hear him calling June's name. It was all very bizarre and compelling viewing. Larna recognised the route he'd taken and whispered, "No, no, no! Don't follow that path!" But he did, still calling for his missing sister-in-law. Every so often he put a hand to his ear, listened, then charged forward excited by something or somebody he had heard.

Screwing up her eyes and leaning as close as she dared to her grandmother without touching her, Larna scoured the forest for anything out of the ordinary. And there it was, a shadowy figure darting from tree to tree. Edsel! A very young and small Edsel, moving so fast he was barely visible. Unless you were actually looking for him. The viewers had an idea what was going to happen next and, from then on, they watched with dread. The scene unfolding was almost identical to what happened to Larna. Only this time, there was fruit on the tree, not paper messages. Somewhere en route, Zebedia must have lost his lunch and was very hungry. So he walked to the tree and was about to pick a fruit when the ground opened, took him down and closed on top of him – a terrifyingly familiar sight for Larna.

They thought that was the end. They stared at the black cloud above the disc, waiting for it to disappear. But it didn't. Instead, a final fragment of a scene became visible – Zebedia's hands touching 'glow' stones as he pulled himself out of the water. The disc also memorised faint pictures of the dark cave as it moved in Zebedia's breast pocket with each frightened step.

"Where are you, Drisco?" was Larna's silent plea.

Her heart lifted as lights began to bob up and down in one of the tunnels, getting brighter and brighter. But, instead of the Undines, an army of Boggrets marched into the huge cave. Heading straight for Zebedia. The memory of their stench made Larna gag and automatically pinched her nose against the long-gone smell. Zebedia tried in vain to crawl back into the pool, but must have been hurt pretty badly because he didn't quite make it. The Boggrets dragged him away from the water, threatening with club-like spears and shoving fire torches in front of his face. Thankfully none touched, but his hair and bushy eyebrows were singed. Becoming bored, their leader – probably Edsel's uncle, Killian – turned away signalling the end of their sport and that the prisoner was to be taken with them. Alive. Face down, Zebedia was dragged into a tunnel by two Boggrets and along the way the photo-disc fell out of his pocket unnoticed. The final shot was of Zebedia's heels as they disappeared from view. Then nothing. Had it shut itself down? Suddenly it lit up again. Thousands of dots like tiny stars partially illuminated the cave and captured a dimly-lit figure huddled between two large boulders. There didn't appear to be any sign of life. Annie's hands spread out seeking support. She went deathly pale and whispered her sister's name, "June!"

The picture flickered and died again. Everyone held their

breath in anticipation of further activity in the disc. Sure enough, it gradually came back to life. The Lumins glowed again as the disc captured a creature slithering out of the water. Unseen hands picked up the disc and carried it back into the lake. There were no further pictures.

Annie fainted, dropping like a stone before anyone could catch her. Chet and Aron picked her up and placed her on Larna's bed, fanning with their hands until she started to regain consciousness. "Don't worry about mum," said Chet. "She'll be alright, once she gets over the shock. Besides, isn't it time you left?"

Hurriedly, Larna and Aron bade Chet and his mother goodbye and returned downstairs via the moving step. Neve stayed behind for a few more minutes with Tibs in order to pass on some comforting words to Annie. Brother and sister waited outside in the garden in complete silence. Neither had anything to say, constructive or otherwise. Eventually, their grandmother appeared. "This was supposed to be your holiday," she sighed. "Your mother won't be very happy with me if you're tired and grumpy in the morning when she picks you up."

Aron and Larna just stood there, saying nothing. Learning the grim fate of Annie's husband and June had taken the gloss off the prospect of going home. Tiblou and Violet joined them. "Mum's going to be fine. The shock is beginning to wear off. She sends you her love and deepest gratitude for everything. At least we now know what happened to Aunty June and Papa Zeb."
A harassed Chet came down alone. "We're going to have our hands full, brother."

Tibs frowned. "Why?"

"Mum wants us to form a search party. Go underground and look for Dad, if he's still alive. She won't listen to reason right now, but she will in time. I hope."

Shutting her eyes in dismay, Larna hoped Annie wouldn't put anyone in danger, now or in the future. After all, she had had first-hand experience of the underworld and it still terrified her.

"To be on the safe side, put Edsel's wand in a secure place, Tiblou," advised Neve. "The evil creature could still find out where it is and wreak havoc if he got his hands on it." So the young wizard took the smooth black wand and held it at arms' length between his two hands.

"I'm not sure what spell to use," he murmured.

"You must have more confidence in yourself, dear," said Neve, patiently. "You've shown great skill already in the way you've defeated Edsel. Trust your new powers. Make them work for you in the way you want."

"Okay, I will," replied Tibs, but his face showed he wasn't as confident as he sounded. He muttered a few strange words and, with a whooshing noise, the wand faded in and out of view before disappearing completely.

"There!" he said with obvious relief. "I've made Edsel's wand disappear, so the monster can't possibly find it." Then under his breath he added, "I hope."

Satisfied the wand was safely hidden, Neve finally announced it was time for them to go. She asked Tibs and Violet to join forces and whisk them across to the geocache spot where they could jump from this dimension back into theirs. The travellers moved at speed to the clearing where Clementine was waiting for them.

"I've been here for ages. What kept you? The key doesn't have everlasting life. If you don't get a move on, you could be stuck here for years." That galvanized them into a round of frenzied hugs, goodbyes, thank yous, and miss yous. Aron insisted on shaking hands, not hugging.

"Are you ready, you two?" asked Clementine.

They said they were. She stood to one side.

"What about you, Yaya? Aren't you coming as well?"

"Don't worry about me," she answered with a smile. "I have my own method of transportation. I'll be waiting for you at the other end."

As before, the jewelled key reappeared in Larna's pocket and began to agitate. She looked up and saw a shooting star in the night sky and thought of Balgaire. At first she thought he was making his final, final appearance. But there was something urgent about the way the light pulsated from the comet. It looked like a warning – a flashing danger sign. Was Balgaire trying to tell them something was wrong? If so, what could it be? Shrugging her shoulders, Larna looked down again and found their grandmother had already disappeared. Now it was their turn, before it was too late.

CHAPTER THIRTY-TWO

L arna and Aron found their grandmother and Clement waiting for them in the clearing. There was a slight breeze rustling the leaves and a freshness in the air as if it had been raining.

"Welcome back, you two." Clem said.

"It's great to be home." Larna was bursting with relief

"No place like it. Nice to travel, but good to come back again, don't ya know."

"Right on!" agreed Aron. High fives with Clem.

"Yaya, what's happened to your robes?" She was dressed in her ordinary, everyday clothes of their time. Neve tut-tutted. "Come on, I can't swan around in those here. People would think I'd gone batty." She began to laugh and slowly walked away.

Clement held out his hand to Larna. "Haven't you forgotten something?"

"No, what?"

He pointed to the key. "That!"

"Don't we get to look after it?"

"No, I'm afraid not. That's my job. It must be returned to where you found it."

He picked up the geocache box and held it out.

"Can we use it again?"

"Of course you can." The old man grinned. "If you can find it." He softened. "Neve is a Superior White Witch and a member of The Grand Council. It is your birthright." He looked chuffed to bits, full of his own importance. "That gives you the right. But, heed my warning; you can only use the key in a responsible manner. Not for personal amusement or to hurt or harm others. Do you understand?"

In silence they nodded and Larna placed the key back in the box. She looked to see how far their grandmother was ahead of them and, when they glanced back to wish Clement goodbye, he'd vanished. So had the geocache box. And so had the spot in the clearing where it had been buried.

Aron started to run to catch up with his gran, but remembered his sister's disability and changed his mind. Instead he helped Larna to walk as fast as she was able until they caught up with Neve and then walked either side of her the rest of the way to Blithe Cottage. The garden gate swung open of its own accord and silently closed behind them, a reminder that there was still magic in the air emanating from their grandmother. She stopped outside the front door.

"Before we go inside, I have to say how proud I am of both of you. What you have achieved in the last few days, in spite of great personal danger, is remarkable. I have to confess though that in the beginning I was against it. I feared I may lose you, but was overruled by the Grand High Council. Thankfully, it has all worked out as planned. Even losing Balgaire was a possibility."

Then in the ensuing silence Neve lead her grandchildren into the cottage.

* * *

They were let off from having a bath or a shower as long as they cleaned their teeth before getting into bed. They felt shattered, but they couldn't resist carrying out a full post-mortem of what had happened to them.

"Put out the light and go to sleep," Neve called up halfway through their analysis.

Aron was reluctant to go to his own room. As he reached the door, Larna turned to switch off her bedside lamp. Out of the corner of her eye, she saw something move. She shot up and looked around. Nothing seemed out of place, so she prepared to snuggle down again. There it was again! A shadow, moving like lightning, then stillness. She sat bolt upright and tried to remember where she had seen whatever it was.

Back under the covers, her brain still wouldn't let her relax. Untangling the sheets from one of the callipers, she crawled out, sat on the end of the bed and studied the wall painting, section by section. It bore a remarkable likeness to... suddenly, it hit her right between the eyes! This was no ordinary picture. This was the future from which she and her brother had just returned. It showed Tiblou's new house, Uncle Roger's Kitchen Café and Cai, sitting on the ground beside the Major Oak – with a sad expression, clearly looking for someone. Was it her? Startled, Larna blinked hard and sat up straight. Surely not, she thought, and then her eye spotted something which she knew had not been there when they came to bed. It was in a corner of the painting – a smooth black wand that was pulsating with a faint light, like Balgaire's comet only much weaker.

Aron heard Larna's loud cry and re-joined his sister on the bed. Together they stared at the bottom right-hand corner. Then something made Larna ask Aron to fetch her jacket. She shoved her hand deep into one of the pockets and pulled out Edsel's wand! It had incorrectly been sent there by Tiblou's spell.

"What's this doing here?" she gasped, dropping it like a hot potato.

"Now we're in trouble," cried Aron. "I think we should tell Yaya."

Larna anxiously bit her bottom lip, deep in thought "No, I don't. This is all my fault." She moaned.

"How do you work that one out?" Aron asked.

"I don't know, but for some reason I still feel it's my fault."

"Well, I think you're stupid. You're over reacting."

Larna ignored him. She snatched up the wand and made for the door.

"Where are you going?" called Aron.

"To hide this," she whispered. "Yaya has been through enough. And if this is my fault, then it's my problem."

They came to the conclusion that the safest thing would be to temporarily bury the wand as far from Blithe Cottage as possible. Until they could fathom out what to do with it. It needed to be enclosed in metal so its power would not radiate through the ground and give away its position. So Aron sneaked downstairs and returned with one of Neve's big old-fashioned biscuit tins.

"This was the only one not full," he puffed. Opening the tin he took out a large bar of yellow soap that smelt like the caretaker's room at school. "I thought, if we melted it a bit so it would stick to the bottom of the tin, we could shove the wand into the middle." He looked at Larna, waiting for the penny to drop, "So it won't rattle when we go out to bury it."

"Yeah! Good thinking!"

They took the soap to the bathroom, half-filled the basin with very hot water and dropped it in, waiting until it was soft enough to work. Pulling the plug, the water drained away leaving a gooey blob. After letting the block cool for a few seconds so they could handle it, Aron picked it up and with help from his sister shoved the wand through the centre. Then they packed it tightly in the box and secured the lid.

Back in the bedroom, Larna found one of her old school ties in her bedside drawer and wound it round the biscuit tin. Making it safe for all time, she hoped.

"Now let's get this thing out of Yaya's house. Just in case."

It took a long time to leave the cottage, Larna being forced to lean on Aron most of the time. They helped themselves to a torch from under the stairs and one of their grandmother's special gardening spades from the back porch before setting out into the forest. The biscuit tin was under one of Larna's arms, the other arm round her brothers's neck for support. Aron carried the spade and the torch. It was pitch black, eerie and a totally different atmosphere from the woods in broad daylight. Big eyes and hoots made them jump. The tree seemed miles away and took ages to reach. Sitting under it for a few minutes to get their breath back, Aron gave a weary sigh, "I hope this doesn't backfire." He pulled a couple of biscuits out of his pocket and handed one to Larna.

"How?"

"Come back to haunt us for doing our own thing. I still think we should tell Yaya.

"I've told you why not. Now stop talking and start digging!"
Stuffing the last piece of biscuit into his mouth Aron pushed

himself up, chose a reasonably soft patch of earth under the tree and began to dig. When he judged the hole was sufficiently deep, they buried the tin with its powerful contents. Then, in silence, Larna helped Aron backfill as best she could and watched him jump up and down until the mound went flat. Satisfied, they had another few minutes rest to gather their strength before slowly retracing their steps. They were exhausted.

As they walked away Aron turned his head to one side, listening to the usual night noises. "What's that?"

"What's what?" Larna asked.

"Sounds like tapping."

"Probably a woodpecker or something. You're letting your imagination work overtime. Now let's get away from here."

But the damage was done. A seed had been planted. Aron's imaginings kept Larna awake that night, listening for the slightest sound. That, plus the pins and needles in her legs.

* * *

At the breakfast table the following morning, Neve surprised them by casually asking about the missing tin. Aron snorted out a mouthful of juice and Larna donned her best innocent face, pretending to be dumb. They looked at each other and shrugged in resignation.

"What biscuit tin?"

"Have you two learned nothing these past few days?" Neve started to laugh. "It wasn't rocket science. I followed the trail of crumbs up the stairs and guess where it led. If you *must* have a midnight feast in your bedroom, I suggest you don't leave incriminating evidence."

Aron went red, but didn't once mention their nocturnal outing, despite his reservations about it. In a fit of conscience, Larna couldn't let her brother take all the blame. "I had some as well." She admitted.

"What have you done with the tin?"

They had to think fast and Larna was first to come up with a suitable answer, lame though it was. "We'd decided to bury something. Until our next visit." Keeping as close to the truth without confessing to the whole.

"Ah! Future treasure-trove, eh?"

"That's right," said Aron.

Then the hall clock chimed ten, reminding them that their mum would arrive at any minute. Excusing themselves Aron raced upstairs with Larna following at a more sedate pace to clean their teeth and bundle their things into backpacks. Neve followed Larna into her room and sat on the edge of the bed. "Come here, dear, and sit down." She patted the covers, "Sometimes I'm a forgetful old lady. I should have dispensed with these leg irons last night. I'd better do it now before your mother arrives. We don't want to frighten the life out of her now, do we?"

Larna began to tremble. "Do you think it'll be okay?"

"These injuries haven't happened in our time," said Neve, tapping the metal. "It's in the future, light years away. Have a little faith in your old grandmother, yes?" She smiled reassuringly and began to dismantle the callipers.

She was right, as usual. Larna's legs were healed and she rewarded Yaya with the biggest hug and loudest thanks she could muster before slinging her backpack over her shoulder and charging off after Aron. Their mum, Elizabeth, had just arrived and was turning the car around ready to drive straight off. She pipped the horn. In the hall the other three stood, each silently replaying shared memories. Neve was the first to make a move and break the spell saying, "Sadly, it's time to go." She put a hand on each of their shoulders and escorted them out of the cottage.

"Will you answer one question for me?" Larna asked as they walked down the drive towards the car.

"Certainly, if I can."

"Is mum a witch, like you?"

"No love, it sometimes skips a generation."

"Does she know?" Aron chimed in. "What you are."

"I doubt it. There has never been a need to tell her."

"Didn't you ever do any magic for her, even when she was a little girl?"

"Probably, but your mother didn't appear to be aware of it."

Turning, her back to the car so her mum wouldn't hear Larna asked, "So, Yaya, how do *we* find out?"

"Find out what?"

"Whether we have 'the power'. Like you."

Neve began to laugh, heartily. "I've been expecting that one for a long time." She mussed both their hair and with a knowing wink said, "You'll have to wait and see."

Larna had already started dreaming of it as they ran to the car. She failed to hear a distant, ominous knocking coming from the woods...

THE END... *for now...*